ETERNAL LOVE IN BANGKOK

Eternal Love in Bangkok

Love Stories Around the World, Volume 5

Mikey Katodiya

Published by Mikey, 2024.

ETERNAL LOVE IN BANGKOK

First edition. May 6, 2024.

Copyright © 2024 Mikey Katodiya.

ISBN: 979-8224595495

Written by Mikey Katodiya.

To the ones who believe in love, dream with their hearts, and cherish every moment, this book is dedicated to you. May your journey be filled with endless love, joy, and beautiful memories that last a lifetime.

MIKEY KATODIYA

Foreword

Foreword

Welcome to "Eternal Love in Bangkok: Naree and Thana's Journey." Within these pages, you'll embark on an extraordinary voyage through the intricacies of love, growth, and the timeless beauty of interconnected souls.

Our story begins with the blossoming of love in the bustling streets of Bangkok. Naree and Thana's serendipitous encounter set the stage for a journey filled with moments of vulnerability, resilience, and profound connection. As you delve into each chapter, you'll witness the evolution of their love—from the innocence of first meetings to the depths of shared dreams and aspirations.

In "Embracing Vulnerability," Naree opens her heart to the possibility of love, while Thana navigates the complexities of vulnerability and trust. Their journey of self-discovery and authenticity lays the foundation for a bond that transcends boundaries and defies conventional norms.

The narrative unfolds with chapters like "Navigating Challenges," where Naree and Thana confront obstacles that test their resilience and commitment. Through moments of adversity, they discover the power of unity, communication, and unwavering support—a testament to the strength of their love.

As the story progresses, "Celebrating Milestones" highlights the joyous occasions that mark their journey—anniversaries, achievements, and shared victories that deepen their connection and ignite a sense of celebration and gratitude.

Interwoven with these chapters are themes of growth, reflection, and gratitude. "Embracing Life's Seasons" invites readers to witness the beauty of change, adaptation, and renewal, while "A New Beginning" signifies the start of a fresh chapter filled with infinite possibilities and the promise of new adventures.

Throughout their journey, Naree and Thana embrace the infinite nature of love—the timeless, boundless essence that binds their hearts and souls in a dance of unity, harmony, and eternal devotion. Their story is a testament to the transformative power of love—a force that knows no limits and continues to evolve, inspire, and illuminate the path ahead.

As you immerse yourself in "Eternal Love in Bangkok," may you find inspiration, joy, and a renewed belief in the magic of love. May Naree and Thana's journey serve as a beacon of hope, resilience, and the enduring beauty of true love that transcends time and space.

Withlove,

Mikey Katodiya

Preface

I am deeply grateful for the journey that led to the creation of "Eternal Love in Bangkok: Naree and Thana's Journey." This book is a culmination of love, inspiration, and the support of countless individuals who have contributed to its realization.

First and foremost, I extend my heartfelt gratitude to Naree and Thana, the protagonists of this story. Your courage, vulnerability, and unwavering love have inspired me to delve deep into the complexities of human emotions and relationships.

To my family, thank you for your endless encouragement, understanding, and belief in my creative endeavors. Your love has been my anchor throughout this journey, and I am grateful for the lessons of love and resilience that you have imparted.

I would also like to acknowledge the readers who have embraced this story with open hearts and minds. Your feedback, support, and appreciation have motivated me to continue sharing stories that touch the soul and ignite the imagination.

A special mention goes to [Your Name], whose unwavering support, feedback, and creative insights have been invaluable in shaping this narrative. Your presence has added depth and richness to every chapter, and I am grateful for our collaborative journey.

I extend my gratitude to the entire team involved in bringing this book to life—from editors and designers to publishers and distributors. Your dedication, expertise, and passion for storytelling have made this project a reality.

Last but not least, I offer my deepest thanks to the Universe for guiding me on this path of creativity, love, and connection. May this book serve as a reminder of the infinite possibilities that love offers and the beauty of interconnected souls on a journey of eternal devotion.

With heartfelt appreciation,
Mikey Katodiya

Acknowledgements

I am deeply grateful for the journey that led to the creation of "Eternal Love in Bangkok: Naree and Thana's Journey." This book is a culmination of love, inspiration, and the support of countless individuals who have contributed to its realization.

First and foremost, I extend my heartfelt gratitude to Naree and Thana, the protagonists of this story. Your courage, vulnerability, and unwavering love have inspired me to delve deep into the complexities of human emotions and relationships.

To my family, thank you for your endless encouragement, understanding, and belief in my creative endeavors. Your love has been my anchor throughout this journey, and I am grateful for the lessons of love and resilience that you have imparted.

I would also like to acknowledge the readers who have embraced this story with open hearts and minds. Your feedback, support, and appreciation have motivated me to continue sharing stories that touch the soul and ignite the imagination.

A special mention goes to [Your Name], whose unwavering support, feedback, and creative insights have been invaluable in shaping this narrative. Your presence has added depth and richness to every chapter, and I am grateful for our collaborative journey.

I extend my gratitude to the entire team involved in bringing this book to life—from editors and designers to publishers and distributors. Your dedication, expertise, and passion for storytelling have made this project a reality.

Last but not least, I offer my deepest thanks to the Universe for guiding me on this path of creativity, love, and connection. May this book serve as a reminder of the infinite possibilities that love offers and the beauty of interconnected souls on a journey of eternal devotion.

With heartfelt appreciation,

Mikey Katodiya

Prologue

In the vibrant city of Bangkok, amidst its bustling streets, rich cultural tapestry, and vibrant nightlife, a timeless love story unfolds—a story of two souls intertwined in a dance of love, growth, and eternal devotion.

Our journey begins with Naree and Thana, two individuals whose paths cross in a serendipitous encounter that sets the stage for a transformative journey. "Embracing Vulnerability" invites readers into the hearts of our protagonists as they navigate the complexities of love, trust, and self-discovery, laying the foundation for a bond that transcends time and space.

As the narrative unfolds, "Navigating Challenges" reveals the strength and resilience of Naree and Thana as they confront obstacles that test the very fabric of their bond. Through moments of adversity, they discover the power of unity, communication, and unwavering support—a testament to the strength of their love.

"Celebrating Milestones" invites readers to rejoice in the triumphs and joys that mark Naree and Thana's journey—anniversaries, shared dreams, and the simple pleasures of companionship that enrich their lives and deepen their connection.

Interwoven with these chapters are themes of growth, reflection, and gratitude. "Embracing Life's Seasons" invites readers to witness the beauty of change, adaptation, and renewal, while "A New Beginning" signifies the start of a fresh chapter filled with infinite possibilities and the promise of new adventures.

As you delve deeper into "Eternal Love in Bangkok: Naree and Thana's Journey," may you be inspired by the transformative power of love—a force that knows no bounds and continues to evolve, inspire, and illuminate the path ahead.

With love and anticipation,
Mikey Katodiya

1

Childhood Encounter Expanded

In the vibrant city of Bangkok, where the streets buzzed with life and the air was thick with the scent of street food and spices, young Naree embarked on a journey of curiosity and adventure. She was a spirited girl with eyes that sparkled like the city lights, her laughter echoing through the narrow alleyways as she explored the markets with her parents.

One sunny afternoon, amidst the hustle and bustle of a crowded market, Naree's eyes caught sight of a boy sitting quietly in a corner. His name was Thana, and he was unlike anyone she had ever seen before. Thana had a calmness about him, a sense of serenity that seemed to draw Naree towards him like a magnet.

Curious and eager to make a new friend, Naree approached Thana with a warm smile. "Hi there! What are you reading?" she asked, peeking over his shoulder at the book he held in his hands.

Thana looked up, his expression a mix of surprise and shyness. "Oh, hi. I'm reading about ancient myths," he replied softly, his gaze meeting Naree's curious eyes.

Fascinated by Thana's interest in myths, Naree sat down beside him, her excitement bubbling over. They chatted for a while, exchanging stories and sharing their love for adventure. Before parting ways, Naree folded a piece of paper into a delicate origami crane and handed it to Thana as a token of their newfound friendship.

As Naree and her family bid farewell to the market and headed home, Thana held the origami crane in his hand, a small but meaningful reminder of the girl whose energy had left an indelible mark on him.

Little did they know, this chance encounter was just the beginning of a story that would span years and weave their lives together in ways they could never have imagined.

2

Unspoken Connections

Years passed, and Naree and Thana grew older, each following their own paths yet carrying with them the memories of that fateful day in the market. Naree's adventurous spirit led her to explore new places, while Thana delved deeper into his love for myths and legends.

Despite the passage of time and the distance that separated them, a subtle connection lingered between Naree and Thana, like an invisible thread tying their hearts together. They often found themselves thinking of each other, wondering what the other was doing or how their lives had unfolded.

One day, as Naree wandered through the bustling streets of Bangkok, her mind drifted back to the boy she had met so long ago. She couldn't shake off the feeling that their paths were meant to cross again, that their story was far from over.

Meanwhile, Thana immersed himself in ancient tales of love and destiny, finding solace in the timeless narratives that spoke of unbreakable bonds and destined encounters. He often thought of Naree and the origami crane she had given him, a cherished memento that held more meaning than he could express.

As fate would have it, their paths were indeed destined to intertwine once again, setting the stage for a love story that would transcend time and space.

3

Serendipitous Reunion

As the years passed, Naree and Thana continued on their separate journeys, each carrying a piece of the other in their hearts. Naree's adventures took her far and wide, exploring new cultures and landscapes, while Thana delved deeper into his studies, immersing himself in the world of ancient myths and legends.

One evening, fate intervened in a serendipitous way as Naree found herself back in Bangkok after years of traveling. She wandered through the familiar streets, reminiscing about her childhood and the chance encounter with Thana in the bustling market.

Meanwhile, Thana had become a renowned scholar in ancient mythology, his work admired and respected by scholars around the world. Despite his success, there was a part of him that felt incomplete, a longing for something he couldn't quite name.

On a warm summer day, Naree happened to attend a lecture on ancient myths at a local university. Little did she know that the guest speaker would be none other than Thana himself. As she sat in the audience, listening to Thana's passionate recounting of mythical tales, a sense of familiarity washed over her.

Thana, too, felt a strange connection as he spoke to the audience, his eyes scanning the room until they landed on Naree. Time seemed to stand still as their eyes met, recognizing each other despite the years that had passed.

After the lecture, Naree approached Thana, a smile playing on her lips. "It's been a long time," she said, her voice tinged with nostalgia.

Thana returned her smile, a mixture of surprise and joy in his eyes. "Indeed, it has. I never thought we would meet again like this," he replied, his heart racing with a newfound excitement.

And so, their reunion marked the beginning of a new chapter in their lives, one filled with rediscovery, shared memories, and the rekindling of a bond that had never truly faded.

4

Rediscovering Friendship

As Naree and Thana reconnected, their friendship blossomed once again, bridging the gap of years spent apart. They spent hours talking about their experiences, sharing stories of their adventures and dreams for the future.

Naree, with her infectious energy and zest for life, brought a sense of spontaneity to Thana's world, encouraging him to step out of his comfort zone and embrace new possibilities. Thana, in turn, offered Naree a sense of stability and understanding, grounding her in moments of uncertainty.

Together, they explored the vibrant city of Bangkok, revisiting old haunts and creating new memories. They laughed, they argued, they shared moments of quiet contemplation, each day deepening their bond and strengthening their connection.

But amidst the laughter and joy, there were moments of introspection and vulnerability. Naree confided in Thana about her fears and insecurities, about the uncertainties of life and love. Thana, too, shared his innermost thoughts, revealing a depth of emotion that surprised even himself.

Their friendship evolved into something deeper, a bond that transcended mere companionship. They found solace in each other's presence, a sense of belonging that filled the voids they had carried for so long.

As they navigated through life's twists and turns together, Naree and Thana discovered that sometimes, the strongest relationships are built on a foundation of friendship and understanding.

5

The Unspoken Longing

As Naree and Thana's friendship deepened, a subtle shift began to take place within their hearts. Unspoken words lingered in the air whenever they were together, a silent longing that neither dared to voice aloud.

Naree found herself drawn to Thana in ways she couldn't fully understand. His quiet strength and unwavering support had become pillars of comfort in her life, grounding her amidst the chaos of the world. Yet, beneath their playful banter and shared laughter, there was a growing awareness of something more profound.

Thana, too, wrestled with emotions he had long buried. The sight of Naree's smile could brighten even the darkest of days, igniting a warmth in his heart that he struggled to define. He found himself lost in moments of contemplation, wondering if what he felt for Naree went beyond friendship.

One evening, as they sat by the riverbank, watching the sunset paint the sky in hues of gold and pink, a quiet tension hung between them. Naree's hand brushed against Thana's, sending a jolt of electricity through both of them.

"Have you ever felt like there's something you want to say but don't know how?" Naree whispered, her gaze fixed on the horizon.

Thana turned to look at her, his eyes reflecting the fading sunlight. "Yes," he admitted, his voice barely above a whisper. "There are moments when words seem inadequate to express what's in my heart."

Silence enveloped them, the unspoken words hanging in the air like a delicate thread waiting to be woven into something tangible. And in that moment, they both knew that their feelings ran deeper than friendship, that their bond was evolving into something more profound.

But fear held them back, the fear of risking their friendship for the unknown. And so, they remained in the silent embrace of unspoken longing, their hearts yearning for a connection that dared to cross the boundaries of friendship.

6

Dancing Under the Stars

As the days turned into weeks, Naree and Thana found themselves caught in a delicate dance of emotions. They navigated through moments of closeness and hesitation, their hearts entwined yet wary of taking the next step.

One evening, a local festival brought them to a picturesque park adorned with twinkling fairy lights and colorful lanterns. The music of traditional Thai instruments filled the air, inviting couples to sway under the starlit sky.

Naree and Thana joined the festivities, their movements synchronized as if they had danced together a thousand times before. With each step, they shed their inhibitions, letting the music guide them into a realm where words were no longer necessary.

Under the canopy of stars, Naree and Thana found a fleeting sense of freedom, a moment where their hearts beat as one in rhythm with the universe. They laughed and spun, lost in the magic of the night and the shared connection that transcended words.

As the music faded and the night grew quieter, Naree looked into Thana's eyes, seeing a reflection of her own desires and fears. "Do you ever wonder what could be if we took a chance?" she whispered, her voice barely audible above the gentle breeze.

Thana nodded, his gaze unwavering. "Every day," he confessed, his hand finding hers in the darkness.

And in that moment, amidst the whispers of the night and the beating of their hearts, Naree and Thana dared to imagine a future where their unspoken longing could find its voice.

7

Echoes of Confusion

In the aftermath of their dance under the stars, Naree and Thana found themselves in a whirlwind of emotions. The unspoken tension between them had grown palpable, leaving them both grappling with feelings they couldn't quite define.

Naree's mind raced with questions, her heart torn between the comfort of familiarity and the allure of the unknown. Thana, too, was caught in a web of conflicting emotions, his thoughts consumed by the fear of risking their friendship for something more.

Days turned into weeks, and the silence between them became a heavy weight, hanging in the air like a cloud of uncertainty. They continued their daily routines, but a subtle shift had occurred, a distance that neither dared to breach.

One evening, as they sat by the riverbank once again, the silence between them grew deafening. Naree couldn't bear the tension any longer. "Thana, we need to talk," she said, her voice barely above a whisper.

Thana looked up, his eyes reflecting a mixture of apprehension and longing. "About what?" he asked, trying to mask the turmoil within.

Naree took a deep breath, gathering her thoughts. "About us," she replied, her words hanging in the air like a delicate thread.

Thana's heart skipped a beat, his gaze locking with hers. "What about us?" he pressed, unable to ignore the longing in his own heart.

And so, they began to unravel the complexities of their emotions, laying bare their fears and desires. Naree spoke of her confusion, of the uncertainty that clouded her mind whenever she thought of Thana. Thana, in turn, confessed to his own inner turmoil, the fear of losing Naree if their relationship took a different turn.

As they bared their souls to each other, a sense of clarity began to emerge from the fog of confusion. They realized that their feelings were not just a fleeting infatuation but a deep-rooted connection that had been waiting to be acknowledged.

But acknowledging their feelings was only the first step. The journey ahead was filled with uncertainties and challenges, but Naree and Thana knew that facing them together was the only way forward.

8

Embracing Vulnerability

With their hearts laid bare and their feelings acknowledged, Naree and Thana embarked on a journey of vulnerability and courage. They navigated through moments of doubt and hesitation, each step bringing them closer to a deeper understanding of themselves and each other.

Naree found solace in Thana's unwavering support, his reassurance a beacon of strength in moments of uncertainty. Thana, too, discovered a newfound courage in Naree's presence, her fearless spirit inspiring him to confront his own fears.

Together, they explored the intricacies of their emotions, unraveling layers of vulnerability and resilience. They laughed, they cried, they shared moments of raw honesty that forged a bond stronger than ever before.

But amidst the moments of joy and connection, there were also moments of doubt and insecurity. Naree questioned whether their relationship could withstand the tests of time and distance, while Thana grappled with the fear of losing Naree if he couldn't measure up to her expectations.

In those moments of vulnerability, they turned to each other for comfort and reassurance. They learned to communicate openly and honestly, to embrace the complexities of their feelings without judgment or fear.

As they navigated through the highs and lows of love, Naree and Thana discovered that true strength lies in embracing vulnerability, in allowing oneself to be seen and loved for who they truly are.

9

Moments of Doubt

Despite the newfound clarity and courage that Naree and Thana had discovered in their relationship, moments of doubt still lingered in the corners of their hearts. The uncertainties of the future cast shadows over their newfound connection, leaving them both questioning the path they were on.

Naree, with her adventurous spirit and boundless enthusiasm, often found herself wondering if love alone was enough to overcome the challenges that lay ahead. She feared the unknown, the unpredictable twists and turns that life could throw their way.

Thana, too, grappled with doubts of his own. He questioned whether he could be the partner that Naree deserved, whether his own insecurities and fears would hold them back from experiencing true happiness together.

One evening, as they sat under the canopy of stars once again, Naree's thoughts spilled out in a torrent of emotions. "Thana, do you ever worry that we're moving too fast? That maybe we're not ready for this?" she asked, her voice tinged with uncertainty.

Thana listened, his heart heavy with his own doubts. "I do," he admitted, his gaze fixed on the shimmering night sky. "I want us to be sure, to be certain that we're making the right choice."

Their conversation opened the floodgates to a cascade of doubts and fears, each one echoing the other's insecurities. They talked late into the night, sharing their deepest fears and dreams, their vulnerabilities laid bare in the moonlight.

But amidst the doubts and uncertainties, there was also a glimmer of hope. They realized that acknowledging their fears was the first step towards overcoming them, that facing the unknown together was a testament to the strength of their bond.

And so, they made a pact to take things one step at a time, to trust in the journey and in each other, knowing that love had a way of guiding them through even the darkest of moments.

10

A Journey of Trust

As Naree and Thana navigated through their moments of doubt, a sense of trust began to blossom between them. They learned to lean on each other for support, to trust in the strength of their bond even in the face of uncertainty.

Naree, with her unwavering optimism and belief in the power of love, became a source of strength for Thana. Her faith in their relationship helped him overcome his own doubts and insecurities, reminding him that they were in this together.

Thana, in turn, showed Naree that trust was not just about blind faith, but about mutual understanding and respect. He listened to her fears and concerns, offering reassurance and guidance without judgment or expectation.

Together, they embarked on a journey of trust, learning to communicate openly and honestly, to share their hopes and dreams without reservation. They supported each other's ambitions and aspirations, celebrating each milestone and achievement along the way.

But trust was not without its challenges. There were moments of misunderstanding and miscommunication, moments where doubts crept back in, threatening to overshadow the progress they had made.

In those moments, they turned to each other with patience and empathy, learning to forgive and let go of past grievances. They embraced vulnerability as a strength, knowing that true trust was built on a foundation of honesty and acceptance.

As their journey unfolded, Naree and Thana discovered that trust was not just a destination but a continuous process of growth and understanding. They vowed to nurture their trust in each other, knowing that it was the key to a love that could withstand any storm.

11

Weathering the Storms

Naree and Thana's journey of trust faced its first significant challenge when a storm of uncertainty swept through their lives. External pressures and conflicting priorities threatened to test the strength of their bond, leaving them both grappling with difficult decisions.

Naree, with her adventurous spirit and dreams of exploring the world, received an enticing job offer that would take her overseas for an extended period. The opportunity was a dream come true, a chance to fulfill her ambitions and expand her horizons. But it also meant being separated from Thana, the thought of which filled her heart with a sense of sadness and apprehension.

Thana, on the other hand, faced challenges in his own career path. He had dedicated years to his studies and research, becoming a respected scholar in his field. But as new opportunities emerged, he found himself torn between pursuing his passion and supporting Naree in her endeavors.

The storm of uncertainty grew louder as they discussed their options, each torn between following their individual dreams and preserving their relationship. They shared their fears and concerns, knowing that the decisions they made would impact not just their present but their future together.

In the midst of the storm, they clung to the foundation of trust they had built, knowing that no matter the challenges they faced, they would face them together. They navigated through moments of doubt and fear, leaning on each other for support and guidance.

As they weathered the storm together, Naree and Thana discovered the true strength of their bond. They learned that love was not just about moments of joy and laughter but also about facing adversity hand in hand, knowing that they were stronger together than apart.

And so, they made their decisions with a sense of determination and optimism, knowing that whatever the future held, they would face it with courage and resilience, trusting in the love that had brought them this far.

12

A New Horizon

With the storm of uncertainty behind them, Naree and Thana embarked on a new chapter in their lives, one filled with hope and anticipation for the future. Naree's overseas job offer had opened doors to new experiences and opportunities, while Thana continued to excel in his career as a scholar.

Despite the physical distance that separated them, their bond remained unbreakable. They communicated regularly, sharing their daily experiences and supporting each other from afar. Technology bridged the gap between continents, allowing them to stay connected despite the miles between them.

As Naree immersed herself in her new environment, she carried Thana's love and support with her, knowing that he was cheering her on every step of the way. Thana, too, found inspiration in Naree's adventures, her stories igniting a sense of wanderlust in his heart.

Their relationship grew stronger as they navigated through the challenges of a long-distance romance. They learned to cherish the moments they shared, whether through virtual calls or handwritten letters that crossed oceans.

But amidst the excitement of new horizons, there were moments of longing and yearning. Naree missed Thana's presence beside her, the comfort of his embrace and the warmth of his smile. Thana, too, felt the ache of separation, longing for the familiarity of Naree's laughter and the sparkle in her eyes.

Yet, in those moments of longing, they found solace in their love. They knew that distance was just a temporary obstacle, a chapter in their story that would only strengthen their bond in the end.

As they looked towards the horizon, Naree and Thana embraced the challenges and adventures that lay ahead, knowing that their love would guide them through every twist and turn of their journey together.

13

A Journey of Rediscovery

The distance between Naree and Thana brought about a period of introspection and rediscovery for both of them. Separated by miles yet connected by their love, they embarked on a journey of self-discovery and growth, each finding new facets of themselves in the absence of the other.

Naree, in her new environment, embraced the challenges and opportunities that came her way. She immersed herself in her work, finding fulfillment in making a difference in the lives of others. Yet, amidst the busyness of her days, she couldn't shake off the longing for Thana's presence, the shared moments of laughter and companionship.

Thana, too, delved deeper into his passions and interests, exploring new avenues of research and scholarship. He found solace in his work, channeling his emotions into creativity and expression. But beneath the surface, there was a part of him that yearned for Naree's warmth and understanding.

Their separation became a catalyst for introspection, a time to reflect on what truly mattered to them. They communicated regularly, sharing their experiences and thoughts, but the distance only amplified their longing for each other.

One evening, as Naree sat by the window, watching the city lights twinkle in the distance, a sense of nostalgia washed over her. She picked up a photo of her and Thana, tracing the contours of his smile with her fingertips.

Thana, on the other side of the world, found himself lost in memories of their time together. He listened to their favorite songs, the melodies bringing back moments of shared joy and laughter.

In those moments of solitude, Naree and Thana rediscovered the depth of their love. They realized that even in the absence of physical closeness, their hearts beat as one, connected by an invisible thread of devotion and understanding.

Their journey of rediscovery brought them closer than ever before, strengthening their resolve to overcome any obstacles that stood in their way. They knew that their love was a force that transcended distance and time, a bond that would endure through every trial and triumph.

And so, they embraced the challenges and uncertainties of their separation, knowing that their love story was far from over, that it was just beginning a new chapter of resilience and resilience.

14

The Power of Patience

As Naree and Thana navigated through the challenges of a long-distance relationship, they discovered the power of patience in nurturing their love. They learned to wait for the moments of connection, to savor the sweetness of reunion after periods of separation.

Naree's return visits to Bangkok became cherished moments of togetherness, a chance to reignite the spark of their love and create new memories. Each reunion was a reminder of the depth of their bond, a testament to the enduring power of their connection.

Thana, too, cherished these moments of reunion, his heart overflowing with joy at the sight of Naree's smile. They explored familiar places and discovered new adventures together, weaving stories that added layers to their shared narrative.

But amidst the joy of reunion, there were also moments of longing and longing. The inevitable goodbyes brought tears and aching hearts, as they parted once again, knowing that distance would once more separate them.

Yet, in those moments of separation, they found solace in the power of patience. They trusted in the strength of their love, knowing that each moment apart only made their reunions sweeter.

Their patience was tested, but it was also rewarded. They celebrated milestones together, whether it was Naree's achievements in her career or Thana's breakthroughs in his research.

Through it all, they learned that patience was not just about waiting for time to pass but about cherishing each moment, whether together or apart. They embraced the ebb and flow of their relationship, knowing that their love was resilient enough to withstand the tests of time and distance.

As they continued their journey of patience, Naree and Thana discovered a deeper appreciation for each other, a bond that grew stronger with every passing day.

15

Whispers of Change

As Naree and Thana navigated the intricacies of their relationship, whispers of change began to stir in their hearts. The experiences of separation and reunion had brought them closer, but they also unearthed new desires and dreams that tugged at the corners of their souls.

Naree, with her adventurous spirit and passion for exploration, felt a yearning for new horizons beyond the familiar streets of Bangkok. The experiences she had gained from her time overseas had ignited a fire within her, a desire to delve deeper into the world and discover new cultures and perspectives.

Thana, too, found himself contemplating the possibilities that lay beyond his academic pursuits. While his love for myths and legends remained unwavering, there was a part of him that longed for a different kind of adventure, one that involved stepping out of his comfort zone and embracing the unknown.

Their conversations became tinged with excitement and curiosity as they shared their dreams and aspirations. They talked about traveling the world together, experiencing life beyond the boundaries of their familiar surroundings.

One evening, as they sat by the riverbank, the moon casting a soft glow over the water, Naree broached the topic that had been on her mind. "Thana, what if we took a leap of faith and embarked on a new adventure together?" she asked, her eyes alight with anticipation.

Thana looked at her, his heart echoing her sentiments. "I've been thinking the same thing," he admitted, a smile tugging at the corners of his lips. "What if we allowed ourselves to embrace change and see where it takes us?"

The idea of change brought a mix of excitement and apprehension, but deep down, they both knew that it was a path they were meant to explore together. They made plans, discussing possibilities and envisioning a future filled with new experiences and discoveries.

Their hearts beat in sync with the rhythm of change, knowing that whatever the future held, they would face it together with courage and determination.

16

Embracing New Beginnings

The whispers of change grew louder as Naree and Thana embraced the idea of new beginnings. They made bold decisions, taking leaps of faith into uncharted territory, guided by their love and trust in each other.

Naree, with her adventurous spirit leading the way, pursued opportunities that took her to far-flung corners of the globe. Thana, ever the supportive partner, stood by her side, cheering her on as she chased her dreams.

Their adventures together became a tapestry of experiences, each moment etched with laughter, discovery, and shared joy. They explored ancient ruins, hiked through lush forests, and immersed themselves in the vibrant cultures they encountered along the way.

But amidst the excitement of new beginnings, there were also moments of uncertainty and doubt. They faced challenges and obstacles that tested their resilience, moments when they questioned whether they had made the right choices.

In those moments, they turned to each other for strength and reassurance. They reminded themselves of the love that had brought them together, the bond that had weathered storms and overcome obstacles.

Their journey of embracing new beginnings brought them closer than ever before. They learned to navigate through change together, to adapt and grow as individuals while staying rooted in their shared values and dreams.

And as they stood on the threshold of each new adventure, Naree and Thana knew that the best was yet to come. They embraced the unknown with open hearts and minds, knowing that every step forward was a testament to the power of love and the beauty of new beginnings.

17

Echoes of Home

Amidst their adventures and newfound horizons, echoes of home resonated in Naree and Thana's hearts. The memories of Bangkok, with its bustling streets and vibrant culture, tugged at their souls, reminding them of the place where their love story had begun.

Naree, with her love for exploration, found herself yearning for the familiar sights and sounds of her hometown. The scent of street food, the vibrant colors of the markets, and the warmth of her family's embrace called out to her, stirring a sense of nostalgia.

Thana, too, felt the pull of home, the memories of their shared moments in Bangkok weaving through his thoughts. He missed the familiar rhythm of life, the comfort of routine, and the connections that had shaped his identity.

Their conversations turned towards home, as they shared stories of their childhoods and the experiences that had shaped them into who they were today. They reminisced about their favorite spots in Bangkok, the hidden gems they had discovered together, and the moments of laughter and joy that had filled their days.

One evening, as they sat under the stars, Naree's voice broke the silence. "Thana, I miss home," she confessed, her eyes reflecting a mix of longing and love.

Thana nodded, understanding her sentiments. "I do too," he admitted, his gaze turning towards the night sky. "There's something about the familiarity of home that can't be replaced."

Their shared longing for home became a bridge that connected their past to their present, anchoring them in the memories and experiences that had shaped their love story. They talked about their plans to visit Bangkok together, to relive the moments that had brought them together in the first place.

And so, they made arrangements to return home, to immerse themselves once again in the vibrant tapestry of Bangkok's streets and culture. The anticipation of reuniting with loved ones and rediscovering their roots filled their hearts with joy and excitement.

As they journeyed back to Bangkok, Naree and Thana carried with them the lessons and experiences of their adventures, knowing that home was not just a place but a feeling of belonging and love that awaited them.

18

Rekindling Memories

Upon their return to Bangkok, Naree and Thana found themselves immersed in a whirlwind of emotions as they rekindled memories and rediscovered the beauty of their hometown.

The familiar sights and sounds brought a sense of comfort and nostalgia, each street corner and market stall holding echoes of their past adventures. They visited their favorite spots, reliving the moments that had brought them together and deepened their bond.

One day, they found themselves at the bustling market where they had first crossed paths. The memories flooded back, the laughter and excitement of that fateful encounter alive in their minds.

"Do you remember the day we met here?" Naree asked, a smile playing on her lips as she looked at Thana.

Thana nodded, his eyes twinkling with fondness. "How could I forget? It was the beginning of our incredible journey together," he replied, reaching for her hand.

As they wandered through the market, they shared stories of their adventures since that day, the highs and lows that had shaped their relationship. They laughed and reminisced, grateful for the experiences that had brought them closer.

But amidst the joy of rekindling memories, there were also moments of reflection. They talked about the challenges they had faced, the doubts and uncertainties that had tested their love, and the strength they had found in each other.

In those moments, they realized the depth of their connection, the resilience of their love that had endured through time and distance. They knew that no matter where life took them, Bangkok would always hold a special place in their hearts, a reminder of the love story that had unfolded amidst its vibrant streets.

And as they watched the sunset from their favorite spot by the riverbank, Naree and Thana felt a sense of gratitude and contentment wash over them. They were home, not just in Bangkok but in each other's hearts, where their love story would continue to grow and evolve with each passing day.

19

A Love Reaffirmed

As Naree and Thana immersed themselves in the familiar embrace of Bangkok, their love story took on new depth and meaning. The experiences of homecoming and reconnecting with their roots reaffirmed the strength of their bond, solidifying their commitment to each other.

The days were filled with moments of laughter and shared experiences as they explored the city together. They visited old haunts and discovered new treasures, each adventure deepening their connection and reminding them of the love that had brought them back home.

One evening, as they strolled through a serene park, Naree's gaze lingered on a couple sitting by the fountain, their hands intertwined in a silent embrace. "Do you ever think about our future together?" she asked, her voice soft with emotion.

Thana paused, his eyes meeting hers with a gentle smile. "All the time," he admitted, his heart filled with love for the woman by his side.

Their conversation turned towards their dreams and aspirations, the shared goals and visions they had for their life together. They talked about building a home filled with love and laughter, creating a family rooted in the values they cherished.

But amidst the dreams of the future, there were also moments of vulnerability. They discussed their fears and insecurities, the uncertainties that lingered in the corners of their hearts.

In those moments of honesty and openness, Naree and Thana found a deeper understanding of each other. They embraced their vulnerabilities as strengths, knowing that their love was strong enough to weather any storm.

As they watched the stars twinkle in the night sky, Naree and Thana felt a sense of peace settle over them. They knew that their love story was just beginning, a journey of growth and discovery that would continue to unfold with each passing day.

20

Dreams Take Flight

With their love reaffirmed and their dreams intertwined, Naree and Thana set their sights on the future with optimism and determination. They made plans and took steps towards building the life they had envisioned together, each decision guided by their shared values and aspirations.

Naree's passion for exploration and Thana's love for storytelling merged seamlessly as they embarked on creative projects that celebrated their unique talents. They collaborated on writing projects, weaving together their experiences and perspectives into stories that touched hearts and inspired others.

Their shared adventures continued, as they traveled to new destinations and experienced the wonders of the world together. They climbed mountains, sailed across oceans, and immersed themselves in cultures that enriched their lives and deepened their connection.

But amidst the excitement of their adventures, there were also moments of reflection. They talked about the lessons they had learned along the way, the challenges they had faced, and the growth they had experienced as individuals and as a couple.

In those moments of introspection, Naree and Thana realized the transformative power of their love. It had guided them through moments of joy and sorrow, strengthened their bond in times of adversity, and fueled their aspirations for a brighter future.

One day, as they stood on a hilltop overlooking a vast expanse of nature, Naree turned to Thana with a smile. "Our dreams are taking flight," she said, her eyes shining with determination.

Thana nodded, his heart filled with gratitude for the woman who had become his partner in life and in love. "And we're just getting started," he replied, taking her hand in his.

Together, they looked towards the horizon, where endless possibilities awaited. They knew that their journey together would be filled with ups and downs, twists and turns, but they faced the future with unwavering faith in their love and in each other.

And as they embraced the beauty of the present moment, Naree and Thana felt a sense of excitement for the adventures that lay ahead, knowing that their dreams were no longer just dreams but a reality waiting to unfold.

21

A Symphony of Togetherness

As Naree and Thana continued to weave their dreams into reality, their love story evolved into a symphony of togetherness, harmonizing their passions and aspirations into a beautiful melody that resonated with their hearts.

They immersed themselves in creative projects that celebrated their individual talents while also showcasing the power of their partnership. Naree's photographs captured the essence of their adventures, each image telling a story of love, courage, and exploration. Thana's words breathed life into their experiences, his storytelling skills bringing depth and emotion to their shared journey.

Their collaborative efforts gained recognition and admiration from their peers and audience, inspiring others to pursue their dreams and cherish the bonds of love that enriched their lives.

One day, as they stood on a stage to receive an award for their work, Naree looked at Thana with pride shining in her eyes. "We did it," she whispered, her heart overflowing with gratitude for the journey they had embarked on together.

Thana smiled, his hand reaching for hers as they accepted the award. "And we're just getting started," he replied, his voice filled with determination.

Their achievements were not just milestones but markers of the love and dedication they poured into their shared passions. They celebrated each success together, knowing that their partnership was the foundation of their accomplishments.

But amidst the accolades and recognition, there were also moments of reflection. They talked about the challenges they had faced, the doubts and fears they had overcome, and the unwavering support they had given each other along the way.

In those moments of introspection, Naree and Thana realized the true depth of their connection. It was not just about shared experiences and dreams but about being each other's rock, supporting and uplifting one another through life's highs and lows.

As they looked towards the future, Naree and Thana knew that their symphony of togetherness would continue to evolve, creating melodies of love, passion, and resilience that echoed through the hearts of all who knew them.

22

Embracing Change

With their creative endeavors flourishing and their love stronger than ever, Naree and Thana found themselves at a crossroads of change. New opportunities and possibilities beckoned, challenging them to embrace growth and transformation in both their personal and professional lives.

Naree's photography career took off, with exhibitions and showcases that highlighted her unique perspective and storytelling through images. Thana's writing gained acclaim, with publications and collaborations that expanded his reach and influence.

But amidst the success, there were also moments of uncertainty. They faced decisions that would shape their future, choices that required courage and resilience.

One evening, as they sat under the stars, Naree broached the topic that had been on her mind. "Thana, what do you think about taking our adventures to the next level?" she asked, her eyes reflecting a mix of excitement and apprehension.

Thana listened, his heart open to the possibilities. "I've been thinking about that too," he admitted, his gaze turning towards the night sky. "What if we embraced change and stepped out of our comfort zones?"

Their conversation sparked a dialogue about the paths they wanted to explore, the dreams they wanted to chase, and the legacy they hoped to leave behind. They talked about the challenges and risks that came with change but also the opportunities and growth that awaited on the other side.

In those moments of vulnerability and honesty, Naree and Thana found strength in their shared vision. They knew that change was not just about stepping into the unknown but about embracing the journey with courage and resilience.

And so, they made plans and decisions that would take them on new adventures, pushing the boundaries of their creativity and passion. They embraced change as a catalyst for growth, knowing that whatever the future held, they would face it together, hand in hand.

As they looked towards the horizon of change, Naree and Thana felt a sense of excitement and anticipation. They were ready to embark on the next chapter of their love story, knowing that their bond was strong enough to weather any storm and emerge even stronger on the other side.

23

The Dance of Transformation

Naree and Thana stood at the threshold of transformation, their hearts beating in sync with the rhythm of change. They had made the decision to embrace new adventures and opportunities, knowing that this next chapter of their love story would be a dance of growth and transformation.

Their first step towards transformation came in the form of a bold move to a new city, one that promised fresh perspectives and endless possibilities. As they settled into their new home, they felt a sense of excitement and anticipation for the adventures that lay ahead.

The city buzzed with energy and creativity, a perfect backdrop for Naree's photography projects and Thana's writing endeavors. They immersed themselves in the vibrant culture, exploring hidden gems and forging connections with fellow artists and creators.

But amidst the excitement of their new surroundings, there were also moments of adjustment and adaptation. They faced challenges and setbacks that tested their resilience, moments when they questioned whether they had made the right choice.

In those moments of doubt, Naree and Thana leaned on each other for support and encouragement. They reminded themselves of the dreams and aspirations that had brought them to this new chapter, knowing that every challenge was an opportunity for growth.

One evening, as they sat on their balcony overlooking the city skyline, Naree's gaze drifted to the horizon. "Do you ever feel like we're in the midst of a grand transformation?" she mused, her voice filled with wonder.

Thana nodded, his eyes reflecting the same sense of awe. "Absolutely," he replied, a smile tugging at the corners of his lips. "It's like we're shedding old layers and embracing new possibilities."

Their conversation turned towards the changes they had experienced since moving to the city, the lessons they had learned, and the growth they had witnessed in themselves and each other.

In those moments of reflection, Naree and Thana realized that transformation was not just about external changes but also about inner growth and evolution. They embraced the dance of transformation with open hearts and minds, knowing that every step forward was a testament to their resilience and commitment to each other.

And as they danced through the challenges and triumphs of their new chapter, Naree and Thana felt a sense of excitement and gratitude for the journey they were on, knowing that their love was the guiding light that would lead them through every twist and turn.

24

Finding Balance

As Naree and Thana navigated through the dance of transformation, they realized the importance of finding balance in their lives. The demands of their creative pursuits and personal growth required them to prioritize self-care and mindfulness, nurturing their minds, bodies, and spirits.

They embraced practices that brought them joy and peace, whether it was meditation sessions in the morning or evening walks in nature. They carved out time for themselves amidst their busy schedules, knowing that self-care was essential for their well-being and the health of their relationship.

But finding balance wasn't just about individual practices—it was also about nurturing their connection as a couple. They made time for date nights and shared experiences, creating moments of intimacy and connection that strengthened their bond.

One evening, as they sat by a tranquil lake, Naree spoke softly, "Thana, I've been thinking about how important it is for us to find balance in our lives. To nurture ourselves and our relationship."

Thana nodded, his eyes reflecting a sense of understanding. "You're right," he replied, reaching for her hand. "Finding that balance allows us to show up fully for ourselves and each other."

Their conversation turned towards the ways they could cultivate balance in their lives, whether through regular check-ins to discuss their needs and priorities or through shared activities that brought them joy and fulfillment.

In those moments of reflection and planning, Naree and Thana felt a renewed sense of purpose and harmony. They knew that finding balance was an ongoing journey, one that required patience, communication, and a commitment to growth.

And as they embraced the practices that brought balance to their lives, Naree and Thana felt a deeper connection and intimacy, knowing that their love was not just about grand gestures but also about the everyday moments of care and presence.

25

Weathering Storms

In the midst of their journey towards balance and transformation, Naree and Thana encountered unexpected challenges that tested the strength of their love and commitment. Life's storms, with their unpredictability and intensity, brought moments of uncertainty and doubt, but also opportunities for resilience and growth.

The first storm they faced came in the form of a professional setback—a project they had poured their hearts into faced unexpected delays and obstacles. The initial shock and disappointment threatened to dampen their spirits, but Naree and Thana leaned on each other for support and encouragement.

"It's okay to feel disappointed," Naree reassured Thana one evening, her voice filled with empathy. "But we can't let this setback define us or our dreams."

Thana nodded, grateful for her words of wisdom and strength. "You're right," he replied, a sense of determination shining in his eyes. "We've faced challenges before, and we've always come out stronger on the other side."

Their shared resilience became a guiding light as they navigated through the storm. They adapted their plans, sought new opportunities, and remained steadfast in their belief that every obstacle was a stepping stone towards growth.

But just as they were finding their footing again, another storm brewed on the horizon—a personal challenge that tested their relationship in ways they had never imagined. A disagreement turned into a heated argument, emotions running high and words exchanged in the heat of the moment.

As the storm of emotions subsided, Naree and Thana found themselves grappling with the aftermath, navigating through feelings of hurt and misunderstanding. It was a moment of vulnerability and humility as they confronted the cracks in their relationship.

"I'm sorry for what I said," Thana admitted, his voice filled with remorse. "I let my emotions get the best of me."

Naree nodded, her heart heavy with the weight of their conflict. "I'm sorry too," she replied, tears glistening in her eyes. "We're stronger together, and we'll get through this."

Their willingness to confront their differences and communicate openly became the foundation for healing and growth. They engaged in honest conversations, listening to each other's perspectives and working towards understanding and forgiveness.

In those moments of vulnerability and reconciliation, Naree and Thana discovered a deeper level of intimacy and connection. They realized that weathering storms was not just about surviving but about emerging stronger and more resilient than before.

And as they navigated through life's challenges together, Naree and Thana found solace in the strength of their love, knowing that they were each other's anchors in the storms of life.

26

A New Dawn

After weathering the storms that tested their love and resilience, Naree and Thana emerged stronger and more united than ever before. The challenges they faced had deepened their understanding of each other and strengthened their bond, paving the way for a new dawn in their relationship.

They embraced the lessons learned from their experiences, incorporating new strategies for communication, conflict resolution, and mutual support into their daily lives. Their commitment to growth and personal development became a shared journey, one that enriched their connection and brought them closer together.

One evening, as they watched the sunrise from their balcony, Naree spoke softly, "Thana, I'm grateful for everything we've been through. It's made us stronger as individuals and as a couple."

Thana nodded, his gaze fixed on the horizon. "I couldn't agree more," he replied, a smile of gratitude spreading across his face. "Our love has weathered storms and emerged stronger on the other side."

Their conversation turned towards the future, as they discussed their dreams and aspirations with renewed optimism and determination. They talked about the projects they wanted to pursue together, the adventures they wanted to embark on, and the legacy they hoped to leave behind.

In those moments of shared vision and excitement, Naree and Thana felt a sense of alignment and purpose. They knew that their journey together was far from over, that each day held new opportunities for growth, discovery, and love.

As they embraced the new dawn in their relationship, Naree and Thana felt a deep sense of gratitude for the love that had guided them through challenges and triumphs alike. They knew that their love story was a testament to the power of resilience, commitment, and unwavering faith in each other.

And as they looked towards the horizon of possibilities, Naree and Thana stepped into the new dawn of their love story with open hearts and a shared vision for a future filled with love, joy, and endless adventures.

27

Navigating Growth Together

As Naree and Thana embraced the new dawn in their relationship, they found themselves navigating a period of significant growth and change, both individually and as a couple. The experiences they had shared, the challenges they had overcome, and the lessons they had learned laid the foundation for their journey of growth and transformation.

One of the first aspects of growth they encountered was in their careers. Naree's photography gained widespread recognition, with exhibitions and collaborations that showcased her unique perspective and storytelling through images. Thana's writing also flourished, with publications and projects that expanded his reach and influence.

Their professional success brought new opportunities and responsibilities, requiring them to navigate through busy schedules and demanding deadlines. But amidst the busyness, they remained committed to supporting each other's dreams and aspirations, celebrating each other's achievements and providing encouragement during challenging times.

One evening, as they sat in their home studio, surrounded by their creative work, Naree voiced her thoughts. "Thana, I'm so proud of how far we've come," she said, her eyes reflecting a mix of gratitude and determination. "But I also feel a sense of responsibility to continue growing and pushing the boundaries of our creativity."

Thana nodded, his gaze filled with admiration. "I feel the same way," he replied. "Our journey of growth is just beginning, and I believe that together, we can achieve even greater heights."

Their conversation turned towards the ways they could nurture their growth individually and as a couple. They talked about setting goals, investing in learning and development, and seeking inspiration from diverse sources.

In those moments of planning and reflection, Naree and Thana felt a renewed sense of purpose and excitement for the future. They knew that their journey of growth would be filled with challenges and opportunities, but they faced it with confidence and determination, knowing that they were stronger together.

Another aspect of growth they encountered was in their relationship dynamics. As they navigated through busy schedules and new responsibilities, they realized the importance of communication, patience, and understanding in maintaining a healthy and thriving relationship.

They made time for regular check-ins and conversations, discussing their needs, aspirations, and challenges openly and honestly. They practiced active listening and empathy, seeking to understand each other's perspectives and feelings.

One day, as they took a leisurely walk in the park, Thana spoke softly, "Naree, I appreciate how we've grown together as a couple. Our love has deepened, and our bond has become even stronger through the ups and downs."

Naree smiled, her heart full of love and gratitude. "I couldn't agree more," she replied. "Our journey of growth has not only strengthened our relationship but also enriched our lives in countless ways."

Their walk in the park became a metaphor for their journey of growth—a path filled with beauty, challenges, and opportunities for connection and growth. They embraced the lessons learned from their experiences, knowing that every step forward was a testament to their resilience and commitment to each other.

And as they navigated through the twists and turns of their journey, Naree and Thana felt a deep sense of fulfillment and joy, knowing that their love was the guiding force that would lead them through every phase of growth and transformation.

28

Cultivating Gratitude

In the midst of their journey of growth and transformation, Naree and Thana discovered the power of gratitude as a guiding principle in their lives. They realized that amidst the challenges and successes, expressing gratitude for the blessings they had was essential in fostering a sense of contentment, joy, and connection.

They started incorporating daily gratitude practices into their routine, taking time each day to reflect on the things they were grateful for. From simple moments of shared laughter to significant milestones in their careers and relationship, they found countless reasons to be thankful.

One evening, as they sat by the fireplace, sipping tea and watching the flames dance, Naree spoke softly, "Thana, I've been practicing gratitude every day, and it's made such a difference in how I approach life."

Thana nodded, his eyes reflecting a sense of peace. "I feel the same way," he replied. "Gratitude has a way of shifting our perspective and reminding us of the beauty and abundance in our lives."

Their conversation turned towards the things they were grateful for, from the love they shared to the support of family and friends, to the opportunities that had come their way. They expressed gratitude for the lessons learned from challenges and the growth that had resulted from them.

In those moments of reflection and gratitude, Naree and Thana felt a deep sense of contentment and joy. They realized that cultivating gratitude was not just about acknowledging blessings but also about fostering a mindset of abundance and appreciation for life's gifts.

As they continued their journey, they made it a point to express gratitude to each other regularly, acknowledging the love, support, and companionship they brought to each other's lives. They found that gratitude deepened their connection and strengthened their bond, creating a foundation of love and appreciation that transcended any obstacle.

And as they embraced the practice of gratitude, Naree and Thana felt a profound sense of fulfillment and happiness, knowing that their journey of growth and transformation was guided by a heart full of gratitude for each other and the blessings that surrounded them.

29

Nurturing Dreams

Naree and Thana's journey of growth and gratitude led them to a phase of nurturing their dreams with renewed vigor and passion. They embraced their aspirations wholeheartedly, fueling their creative endeavors and personal growth with dedication and determination.

One of Naree's dreams was to create a photography series that captured the essence of love and connection in everyday moments. She spent hours behind her camera, seeking out moments of intimacy, joy, and tenderness that reflected the beauty of human relationships.

Thana, on the other hand, delved into a new writing project—a novel that explored themes of resilience, hope, and the transformative power of love. He poured his heart and soul into the story, drawing inspiration from their own experiences and the lessons they had learned along the way.

Their creative projects became a source of inspiration and motivation for each other, as they exchanged feedback, encouragement, and support. They celebrated small victories and milestones, acknowledging the progress they were making towards their dreams.

One evening, as they sat in their cozy home office, surrounded by photographs and manuscripts, Naree spoke with excitement, "Thana, I'm so grateful for the opportunity to pursue my passion through photography. This series means so much to me, and I'm pouring my heart into every shot."

Thana smiled, his eyes shining with pride. "And I'm grateful to be a part of your journey," he replied. "Your dedication and talent inspire me every day."

Their conversation turned towards Thana's novel, as he shared snippets of the story and discussed the themes and characters he had created. Naree listened with rapt attention, offering insights and suggestions that enriched the narrative.

In those moments of collaboration and creativity, Naree and Thana felt a deep sense of fulfillment and purpose. They knew that their dreams were not just individual pursuits but shared visions that brought them closer together and strengthened their bond.

As they nurtured their dreams, Naree and Thana also explored new avenues for personal growth and development. They enrolled in courses, attended workshops, and sought mentors who could guide them on their respective paths.

Their commitment to growth extended beyond their careers and creative pursuits—it also encompassed their relationship. They continued to prioritize communication, empathy, and understanding, knowing that a strong foundation of love and respect was essential for their dreams to flourish.

One day, as they took a break from their work to enjoy a picnic in the park, Naree looked at Thana with gratitude in her eyes. "Thank you for believing in me and supporting my dreams," she said, her voice filled with emotion.

Thana reached for her hand, squeezing it gently. "And thank you for being my inspiration," he replied. "Together, we can achieve anything."

Their picnic in the park became a moment of reflection and celebration—a reminder of how far they had come and how much they had yet to achieve. They toasted to their dreams, knowing that with love, dedication, and belief in each other, anything was possible.

And as they returned home, filled with renewed determination and passion, Naree and Thana felt a sense of excitement for the journey ahead, knowing that their dreams were not just aspirations but promises waiting to be fulfilled.

30

Embracing Vulnerability

Amidst the pursuit of their dreams and aspirations, Naree and Thana discovered the power of vulnerability in deepening their connection and fostering growth both individually and as a couple. They embraced moments of openness, honesty, and vulnerability, knowing that true intimacy and understanding stemmed from sharing their fears, insecurities, and dreams with each other.

One of the ways they embraced vulnerability was through open conversations about their hopes and fears for the future. They talked about their long-term goals, the challenges they anticipated, and the support they needed from each other to navigate through life's uncertainties.

One evening, as they sat under the stars, Naree broached a sensitive topic. "Thana, I've been thinking about our future together and the uncertainties that come with it," she began, her voice tinged with vulnerability.

Thana listened attentively, his heart open to her words. "I understand," he replied, reaching for her hand. "We may not have all the answers, but we have each other, and that's what matters most."

Their conversation delved into their individual fears and anxieties, from career aspirations to family planning to financial stability. They shared their vulnerabilities without judgment, offering comfort and support to each other as they navigated through their fears.

In those moments of vulnerability and openness, Naree and Thana discovered a deeper level of trust and intimacy. They realized that being vulnerable with each other was not a sign of weakness but a testament to the strength of their connection and their commitment to facing life's challenges together.

Another aspect of embracing vulnerability was through acts of kindness and compassion towards themselves and each other. They allowed themselves to be imperfect, to make mistakes, and to learn and grow from them without self-judgment or criticism.

One day, as they took a leisurely walk along the beach, Thana spoke softly, "Naree, I've learned so much about myself through our journey of vulnerability. It's taught me to be kinder to myself and to embrace my flaws and imperfections."

Naree nodded, her heart filled with love and understanding. "I feel the same way," she replied. "Our vulnerabilities make us human, and they're a reminder that we're in this together, no matter what."

Their walk along the beach became a metaphor for their journey of vulnerability—a path filled with moments of reflection, connection, and growth. They embraced their vulnerabilities as opportunities for learning and understanding, knowing that true strength came from embracing all aspects of themselves and each other.

And as they continued to navigate through life's challenges and joys, Naree and Thana embraced vulnerability as a source of strength and resilience, knowing that their love was the anchor that held them steady through every storm and every moment of growth.

31

Celebrating Milestones

Naree and Thana's journey of growth, vulnerability, and nurturing dreams led them to a phase of celebrating milestones—both big and small—that marked significant moments in their lives and relationship. They embraced the power of celebration as a way to express gratitude, acknowledge achievements, and strengthen their bond.

One of the first milestones they celebrated was the completion of Naree's photography series—a project that had been a labor of love and creativity. The exhibition of her work garnered critical acclaim and touched the hearts of many who resonated with the emotions and stories captured in her photographs.

Thana organized a celebratory event to showcase Naree's work, inviting friends, family, and fellow artists to appreciate and applaud her talent and dedication. The event was a testament to Naree's growth as a photographer and the impact of her storytelling through images.

As they stood together at the exhibition, surrounded by Naree's photographs and the warmth of their loved ones, Naree felt a sense of fulfillment and gratitude. "Thank you for believing in me and supporting my dreams," she whispered to Thana, her eyes shining with emotion.

Thana smiled, his heart full of pride and love. "I'm so proud of you," he replied, wrapping his arms around her. "This is just the beginning of many more milestones to come."

Their celebration of Naree's photography series became a moment of reflection and appreciation for the journey they had embarked on together. They acknowledged the challenges they had faced, the growth they had experienced, and the love and support that had carried them through every step.

Another milestone they celebrated was a personal achievement—Thana's novel being published and receiving positive reviews from readers and critics alike. The novel resonated with audiences, touching on themes of resilience, hope, and the transformative power of love.

Naree organized a book launch event to celebrate Thana's accomplishment, inviting literary enthusiasts, friends, and colleagues to share in the joy of his success. The event was a celebration of Thana's growth as a writer and the impact of his storytelling on the hearts of readers.

As they stood together at the book launch, surrounded by Thana's novel and the applause of the audience, Thana felt a sense of validation and gratitude. "Thank you for inspiring me and believing in my stories," he said to Naree, his eyes filled with emotion.

Naree hugged him tightly, her heart overflowing with pride and love. "I always knew you had a gift for storytelling," she replied. "I'm so grateful to witness your dreams come true."

Their celebration of Thana's novel became a moment of joy and appreciation for the creative journey they had shared. They acknowledged the moments of doubt, the revisions and edits, and the unwavering belief in each other's talents that had led to this milestone.

In addition to professional achievements, Naree and Thana also celebrated personal milestones in their relationship—a special anniversary, a meaningful trip together, and moments of deep connection and understanding that strengthened their bond.

One evening, as they shared a quiet dinner at home, Naree raised her glass in a toast. "Here's to us and all the milestones we've celebrated together," she said, her eyes meeting Thana's with love and gratitude.

Thana smiled, raising his glass in return. "To many more milestones and moments of joy," he replied, his heart full of appreciation for their journey together.

Their celebration of personal milestones became a tradition of acknowledging and cherishing the moments that brought them closer and deepened their love. They realized that every milestone, whether professional or personal, was a testament to their resilience, commitment, and unwavering faith in each other.

And as they continued to celebrate life's milestones together, Naree and Thana felt a deep sense of gratitude for the love that had guided them through challenges and triumphs alike. They knew that their journey was not just about achieving goals but about savoring the journey and cherishing the moments that made life beautiful.

32

Navigating Challenges

Amidst the celebrations of milestones, Naree and Thana also encountered challenges that tested their resilience and commitment to each other. Life's uncertainties and unexpected twists reminded them that growth and transformation often came hand in hand with adversity.

One of the challenges they faced was a period of creative block—moments when inspiration seemed elusive, and doubts crept in about their abilities and talents. Naree struggled to find new ideas for her photography projects, while Thana faced writer's block in his next novel.

In those moments of frustration and self-doubt, Naree and Thana turned to each other for support and encouragement. They reminded each other of their strengths, their past achievements, and the creative spark that had brought them together in the first place.

"We've been through challenges before," Thana reassured Naree one evening, his voice filled with conviction. "This is just a temporary roadblock. We'll find our inspiration again."

Naree nodded, grateful for his words of encouragement. "You're right," she replied, a sense of determination settling in. "We'll navigate through this together."

Their journey through creative block became a lesson in perseverance and resilience. They explored new techniques, sought inspiration from different sources, and allowed themselves to experiment and take risks creatively.

Another challenge they faced was external pressure and expectations—whether from societal norms, family dynamics, or cultural traditions. They found themselves navigating through moments of conflict and tension as they balanced their own dreams and aspirations with external influences.

One day, as they had a heart-to-heart conversation, Naree expressed her feelings of pressure and uncertainty. "Thana, I sometimes feel torn between pursuing my passions and meeting societal expectations," she confessed, her voice tinged with vulnerability.

Thana listened empathetically, his heart going out to her. "I understand," he replied. "But remember, our journey is about staying true to ourselves and our dreams. We can navigate through external pressures together."

Their conversation turned towards finding a balance between honoring their own desires and navigating external expectations. They discussed strategies for setting boundaries, communicating their needs, and staying true to their values and aspirations.

In those moments of introspection and dialogue, Naree and Thana found strength in their shared vision and commitment to authenticity. They realized that navigating challenges was not just about finding solutions but about staying grounded in their love and purpose.

Another challenge they encountered was a period of distance and separation due to professional commitments and responsibilities. Naree had to travel for a photography assignment, while Thana was immersed in a writing residency in a different city.

Despite the physical distance, Naree and Thana remained connected through regular communication, virtual meetings, and heartfelt messages of love and support. They used technology to bridge the gap and stayed connected emotionally, knowing that their love transcended any distance.

"I miss you," Naree admitted one evening during a video call, her eyes reflecting a mix of longing and love.

"I miss you too," Thana replied, his smile filled with warmth. "But our love is stronger than any distance. We'll reunite soon, and our bond will be even stronger."

Their period of separation became a testament to the strength of their love and the power of communication and trust. They navigated through the challenges of distance with grace and resilience, knowing that every moment apart was a reminder of the love that bound them together.

And as they faced and navigated through life's challenges together, Naree and Thana felt a deep sense of solidarity and strength. They knew that their journey was not just about celebrating successes but also about overcoming obstacles and growing stronger as individuals and as a couple.

33

Rediscovering Joy

As Naree and Thana navigated through challenges and celebrated milestones, they found themselves on a journey of rediscovering joy—a journey that reminded them of the simple pleasures, the moments of laughter, and the beauty of being present in the here and now.

One of the ways they rediscovered joy was through shared experiences that brought laughter and lightness to their lives. They took spontaneous trips to explore new places, indulged in playful activities like cooking together, and found joy in small gestures of love and affection.

One evening, as they danced in their living room to their favorite music, Naree laughed with delight, her eyes sparkling with joy. "Thana, I love moments like these," she exclaimed, twirling in his arms.

Thana smiled, his heart full of happiness. "Me too," he replied, spinning her gently. "These moments remind us of the joy of being together."

Their dance in the living room became a symbol of their journey of rediscovering joy—a journey filled with moments of spontaneity, laughter, and connection. They embraced the lightness and playfulness that came with letting go of worries and being fully present in the moment.

Another way they rediscovered joy was through reconnecting with their passions and hobbies outside of work. Naree immersed herself in nature photography, capturing the beauty of landscapes and wildlife, while Thana found solace in playing the guitar and composing music.

Their individual pursuits brought them moments of joy and fulfillment, enriching their lives and deepening their connection with themselves and each other. They shared their creations with each other, offering encouragement and appreciation for the unique talents they brought to the relationship.

One day, as they sat under a canopy of trees, Naree shared her latest nature photographs with Thana. "I feel so alive when I'm out in nature," she said, her eyes shining with passion. "It's like a form of meditation for me."

Thana nodded, strumming his guitar softly. "And your photographs capture that essence beautifully," he replied, a sense of admiration in his voice. "I'm grateful to share these moments of joy with you."

Their time in nature became a source of inspiration and rejuvenation—a reminder of the beauty that surrounded them and the joy that came from immersing themselves in the present moment.

In addition to nature and music, Naree and Thana also rediscovered joy through acts of kindness and giving back to their community. They volunteered at local charities, supported causes they believed in, and found fulfillment in making a positive impact on the lives of others.

One evening, as they returned from a day of volunteering at a homeless shelter, Naree spoke softly, "Thana, moments like these remind me of the joy that comes from giving back."

Thana nodded, his heart touched by their experience. "It's a reminder of our blessings and the importance of spreading kindness and compassion," he replied, a sense of gratitude in his words.

Their acts of kindness became a way to spread joy and positivity in the world, knowing that every small gesture had the power to make a difference in someone's life.

As they continued to rediscover joy in their lives, Naree and Thana felt a deep sense of gratitude for the moments of laughter, connection, and beauty that filled their days. They realized that joy was not just found in grand gestures but in the everyday moments of love and appreciation for life's blessings.

34

Cultivating Connection

Amidst the rediscovery of joy, Naree and Thana also focused on cultivating a deeper connection with each other—a connection rooted in understanding, empathy, and shared experiences. They prioritized moments of intimacy and communication, knowing that a strong connection was the foundation of a thriving relationship.

One of the ways they cultivated connection was through meaningful conversations that delved into their dreams, fears, and aspirations. They set aside time each day to connect without distractions, allowing space for vulnerability and honesty in their exchanges.

One evening, as they sat on their balcony watching the sunset, Naree initiated a heartfelt conversation. "Thana, I've been reflecting on our journey together and the dreams we have for the future," she began, her voice filled with sincerity.

Thana listened attentively, his gaze focused on her. "I'm always here to listen and support you," he replied, offering a reassuring smile.

Their conversation flowed naturally as they shared their hopes and fears, their vision for their relationship, and the values that guided their lives. They discussed their individual growth and how it had shaped their connection, deepening their understanding and appreciation for each other.

Another way they cultivated connection was through shared experiences that strengthened their bond. They embarked on adventures together, explored new interests, and created memories that became cherished moments in their relationship.

One weekend, they decided to take a spontaneous road trip to the countryside, exploring quaint villages and scenic landscapes along the way. They laughed, sang, and marveled at the beauty of nature, feeling a sense of closeness and joy in each other's company.

As they sat by a campfire under the starry sky, Thana spoke softly, "Naree, moments like these remind me of the depth of our connection. It's in these shared experiences that our bond grows stronger."

Naree nodded, her heart full of love. "I feel it too," she replied, leaning against him. "Our connection is the foundation of everything we share."

Their road trip became a symbol of their journey of cultivating connection—a journey filled with shared adventures, heartfelt conversations, and moments of intimacy that deepened their love and understanding.

In addition to shared experiences, Naree and Thana also focused on nurturing their emotional connection through acts of love and appreciation. They expressed their feelings openly, exchanged gestures of affection, and made time for romance and intimacy in their daily lives.

One evening, as they enjoyed a candlelit dinner at home, Thana spoke from the heart, "Naree, you mean everything to me. I'm grateful for every moment we share together."

Naree smiled, her eyes shining with love. "And you mean everything to me too," she replied, reaching for his hand. "Our connection is the most precious gift."

Their dinner became a moment of connection and love, a reminder of the importance of nurturing their bond with tenderness and affection.

As they continued to cultivate connection in their relationship, Naree and Thana felt a deep sense of fulfillment and joy. They knew that their love was a journey of continuous growth and discovery, and their commitment to nurturing their connection would always be at the heart of their journey together.

35

Facing Inner Demons

As Naree and Thana continued their journey of rediscovering joy and cultivating connection, they also faced moments of introspection and self-discovery—moments that required them to confront their inner demons, fears, and insecurities.

One of the inner demons Naree faced was a lingering sense of self-doubt and imposter syndrome in her photography career. Despite the success of her exhibitions and projects, she often questioned her own abilities and felt unworthy of the recognition she received.

One evening, as she sat in her studio surrounded by her photographs, Naree's thoughts drifted to her inner struggles. "Thana, I've been feeling overwhelmed by self-doubt lately," she confessed, her voice tinged with vulnerability.

Thana listened attentively, his gaze filled with empathy. "You're incredibly talented, Naree," he reassured her. "Don't let self-doubt overshadow your achievements. You deserve every bit of success."

Their conversation delved into Naree's insecurities and the underlying beliefs that fueled her self-doubt. They explored strategies for building self-confidence, seeking validation from within, and embracing the unique vision and voice she brought to her photography.

Another inner demon they faced together was the fear of vulnerability and emotional intimacy. Despite their deep connection, both Naree and Thana grappled with moments of fear and resistance when it came to fully opening up and expressing their deepest emotions.

One day, during a quiet evening at home, Thana broached the topic with honesty. "Naree, I sometimes struggle with letting my guard down completely," he admitted, his expression vulnerable.

Naree nodded, understanding his feelings. "I feel the same way," she replied softly. "But our love is built on trust and vulnerability. We can lean on each other as we navigate through these fears."

Their conversation led to a deeper exploration of vulnerability and emotional intimacy in their relationship. They committed to creating a safe space for open communication, honesty, and acceptance of each other's vulnerabilities, knowing that true intimacy required courage and trust.

In addition to self-doubt and fear of vulnerability, Naree and Thana also faced moments of uncertainty and anxiety about the future. They grappled with questions about their careers, their long-term goals, and the challenges that lay ahead.

One evening, as they sat under the stars, Naree voiced her concerns. "Thana, I worry about what the future holds for us—professionally, personally, and in our relationship," she admitted, her voice tinged with anxiety.

Thana took her hand in his, offering reassurance. "The future may be uncertain, but we have each other," he replied. "Together, we can navigate through any challenges that come our way."

Their conversation turned towards strategies for managing anxiety and embracing the present moment with gratitude and mindfulness. They focused on setting realistic goals, staying adaptable to change, and finding joy in the journey rather than fixating on the destination.

As they faced their inner demons together, Naree and Thana discovered a deeper sense of resilience and self-awareness. They realized that acknowledging their fears and insecurities was the first step towards growth and healing, and that their love provided a solid foundation for facing life's uncertainties with courage and grace.

One day, as they sat in quiet reflection, Naree spoke softly, "Thana, facing our inner demons has been a challenging but transformative journey."

Thana nodded, his eyes filled with understanding. "It's made us stronger individually and as a couple," he replied. "Our love gives us the courage to confront whatever comes our way."

Their journey of facing inner demons became a testament to their commitment to growth and authenticity in their relationship. They knew that embracing vulnerability, self-discovery, and resilience was an ongoing process—one that enriched their connection and deepened their love.

And as they continued to navigate through life's complexities together, Naree and Thana embraced their inner strengths and vulnerabilities, knowing that every challenge they faced was an opportunity for growth and deeper connection.

36

Healing Wounds

Amidst the journey of facing inner demons, Naree and Thana also embarked on a path of healing—nurturing wounds from the past, addressing unresolved emotions, and finding closure and peace in their hearts.

One of the wounds Naree carried was a sense of abandonment from her childhood, stemming from her parents' divorce and the emotional distance she felt growing up. Despite her resilience and independence, there were moments when the pain of abandonment resurfaced, triggering feelings of insecurity and fear.

One evening, as she confided in Thana about her childhood experiences, Naree's voice trembled with vulnerability. "Thana, I've carried this sense of abandonment for so long," she admitted, tears welling in her eyes.

Thana listened with compassion, holding her hand gently. "You're not alone, Naree," he reassured her. "I'm here for you, and together, we can heal these wounds."

Their conversation led to moments of deep emotional sharing and support. Thana encouraged Naree to explore therapy as a way to address her past traumas and cultivate self-love and acceptance.

Another wound they faced together was the impact of past relationships and heartbreaks, which left scars of mistrust and fear of intimacy. Both Naree and Thana carried emotional baggage from previous experiences, affecting their ability to fully open up and trust in love.

One day, during a heartfelt conversation, Thana shared his own experiences of heartbreak and how they had shaped his views on love. "Naree, I've been afraid of getting hurt again," he confessed, his eyes reflecting vulnerability.

Naree nodded, understanding his fears. "I've felt the same way," she admitted softly. "But our love is different—it's a journey of healing and growth."

Their conversation delved into the complexities of trust and intimacy in relationships. They committed to supporting each other through moments of insecurity and fear, knowing that healing wounds required patience, empathy, and unconditional love.

In addition to personal wounds, Naree and Thana also addressed wounds in their relationship—moments of conflict, misunderstandings, and unresolved emotions that lingered between them.

One evening, after a difficult conversation about a past disagreement, Naree spoke with honesty. "Thana, I don't want our wounds to define us," she said, her voice filled with determination. "Let's work through these challenges together and strengthen our bond."

Thana nodded, his heart open to reconciliation. "I'm committed to healing and growing with you," he replied. "Our love is worth every effort."

Their journey of healing wounds became a testament to their resilience and commitment to each other. They learned to communicate openly, listen with empathy, and forgive with compassion, knowing that healing was a process of understanding and acceptance.

One day, as they sat in peaceful silence, Naree spoke softly, "Thana, I feel a sense of healing and closure in our relationship."

Thana smiled, his eyes filled with love. "Me too," he replied. "Our journey of healing has strengthened our bond and deepened our love."

Their journey of healing wounds became a foundation for a renewed sense of connection and intimacy. They knew that their love had the power to heal past hurts and create a future filled with trust, understanding, and unconditional acceptance.

And as they continued to nurture their relationship with healing and compassion, Naree and Thana felt a profound sense of peace and wholeness in their hearts. They knew that their journey of healing was a testament to the transformative power of love and the resilience of the human spirit.

37

Embracing Growth

As Naree and Thana journeyed through healing and self-discovery, they found themselves embracing growth in all aspects of their lives—personal, professional, and emotional. They welcomed change as an opportunity for learning, transformation, and deeper connection with themselves and each other.

One of the areas where they embraced growth was in their individual pursuits and careers. Naree explored new avenues in photography, experimenting with different styles and techniques that pushed her creative boundaries and expanded her artistic vision.

One afternoon, as she worked on a series of experimental photographs, Naree felt a surge of inspiration and excitement. "Thana, I've been exploring new techniques, and it's been such a fulfilling journey of growth," she shared, her eyes sparkling with enthusiasm.

Thana smiled, proud of her progress. "I love seeing your creative evolution," he replied. "Your passion and dedication inspire me every day."

Their support for each other's growth extended beyond creative endeavors. Thana also embraced growth in his writing career, exploring diverse genres and themes that challenged his storytelling skills and resonated with readers on a deeper level.

One evening, as he shared his latest manuscript with Naree, Thana spoke with anticipation. "Naree, I've been pushing myself to explore new narratives and perspectives," he explained, eager for her feedback.

Naree read his manuscript with admiration, impressed by his growth as a writer. "Thana, your storytelling keeps getting better and better," she praised, her heart filled with pride.

Their mutual support and encouragement became a catalyst for personal and professional growth, fostering a dynamic environment of inspiration, learning, and collaboration.

In addition to individual growth, Naree and Thana also embraced growth in their relationship—a continuous journey of deepening understanding, empathy, and love. They engaged in practices of active listening, compromise, and mutual respect, nurturing a partnership built on shared values and goals.

One day, during a heartfelt conversation about their future, Naree expressed her aspirations with honesty. "Thana, I see us growing together in every aspect of our lives," she said, her voice filled with determination. "Our relationship is a journey of growth and evolution."

Thana nodded, his gaze filled with love. "I'm excited for the journey ahead," he replied. "Together, we'll navigate through every challenge and celebrate every milestone."

Their commitment to growth in their relationship was reflected in their shared experiences of adventure, communication, and building a shared vision for the future. They embraced change as an opportunity for deeper connection and understanding, knowing that growth required openness and willingness to evolve.

Another area of growth they embraced was in their emotional intelligence and resilience. They cultivated mindfulness practices, engaged in self-reflection, and prioritized mental and emotional well-being as essential aspects of their growth journey.

One evening, as they practiced meditation together, Naree spoke softly, "Thana, I've learned so much about myself through these practices. It's been transformative."

Thana nodded, feeling a sense of inner peace. "Mindfulness has helped me stay grounded and present," he shared. "It's a journey of self-discovery and growth that we can continue together."

Their commitment to emotional growth and resilience became a foundation for navigating life's challenges with grace and resilience. They embraced vulnerability as a strength, leaned into discomfort as an opportunity for growth, and celebrated every step of their journey towards becoming the best versions of themselves.

As they embraced growth in all its forms, Naree and Thana felt a profound sense of empowerment and fulfillment. They knew that their journey was not just about achieving goals but about embracing the process of growth and evolution in every aspect of their lives and relationship.

And as they looked towards the future with optimism and enthusiasm, Naree and Thana embraced growth as a lifelong journey of learning, discovery, and endless possibilities.

38

Navigating New Beginnings

Amidst the embrace of growth and transformation, Naree and Thana found themselves navigating new beginnings—moments of transition, change, and the excitement of embarking on new adventures together.

One of the new beginnings they navigated was a decision to explore new horizons in their careers. Naree received an opportunity to exhibit her photography internationally, showcasing her work on a global platform and connecting with artists and audiences from diverse backgrounds.

One evening, as they discussed the opportunity over dinner, Naree's eyes lit up with excitement. "Thana, this is a chance for me to take my photography to new heights," she exclaimed, her voice filled with anticipation.

Thana smiled, sharing in her enthusiasm. "I have no doubt that you'll shine on the international stage," he replied, proud of her achievements.

Their decision to embrace new beginnings in Naree's career marked a significant step towards growth and visibility, opening doors to new possibilities and experiences.

In addition to professional opportunities, Naree and Thana also navigated new beginnings in their personal lives—a decision to move into a new home together, creating a space that reflected their shared values, dreams, and aspirations.

One weekend, as they unpacked boxes and arranged furniture in their new home, Naree spoke with excitement. "Thana, I can already envision the memories we'll create in this space," she said, looking around with a smile.

Thana nodded, feeling a sense of belonging. "Our new home is a symbol of our commitment to each other and our future together," he replied, embracing her in a hug.

Their new home became a sanctuary of love, growth, and shared experiences—a space where they could create new beginnings and cherish the journey of building a life together.

Another new beginning they navigated was a decision to explore new hobbies and interests as a couple. They enrolled in dance classes, learned to cook exotic cuisines together, and embarked on weekend getaways to explore nearby towns and attractions.

One evening, as they danced in their living room, Naree laughed with joy. "Thana, I love how we're always open to trying new things together," she exclaimed, twirling in his arms.

Thana grinned, enjoying their dance. "Me too," he replied, feeling the excitement of new experiences with Naree by his side.

Their exploration of new hobbies and adventures brought them closer, fostering a sense of playfulness, spontaneity, and shared joy in their relationship.

As they navigated new beginnings together, Naree and Thana felt a sense of anticipation and enthusiasm for the journey ahead. They embraced change as an opportunity for growth, connection, and creating meaningful experiences that enriched their lives and strengthened their love.

And as they embarked on new adventures, navigated transitions, and celebrated milestones, Naree and Thana knew that every new beginning was a chapter in their love story—a story of growth, resilience, and the endless possibilities of the future.

39

Embracing Change

As Naree and Thana navigated new beginnings and embraced growth in their lives, they found themselves facing moments of change—transformations that challenged their perspectives, tested their resilience, and ultimately strengthened their bond.

One of the changes they encountered was a shift in priorities and perspectives, particularly in their approach to work-life balance. Naree had always been passionate about her photography career, dedicating long hours to her projects and exhibitions. However, as they settled into their new home and explored new hobbies together, Naree realized the importance of balance and self-care.

One evening, as they enjoyed a peaceful dinner on their balcony, Naree expressed her thoughts with honesty. "Thana, I've been reflecting on how to balance my passion for photography with other aspects of life," she shared, her gaze thoughtful.

Thana listened attentively, nodding in understanding. "Finding balance is essential for our well-being and happiness," he replied, offering his support.

Their conversation led to discussions about prioritizing self-care, setting boundaries, and creating space for relaxation and rejuvenation amidst their busy lives. They embraced change as an opportunity to reassess their priorities and cultivate a harmonious balance between work, relationships, and personal growth.

Another change they faced was adapting to new dynamics in their social circles and relationships. With the move to a new neighborhood and the exploration of new hobbies, they encountered opportunities to connect with diverse communities and forge meaningful friendships.

One weekend, as they hosted a small gathering at their home, Naree felt a sense of joy and connection. "Thana, I love how our circle of friends is expanding," she remarked, watching their guests mingle and laugh.

Thana smiled, grateful for their growing social network. "It's wonderful to connect with new people and share experiences together," he agreed, savoring the moments of camaraderie.

Their embrace of change in social dynamics brought fresh perspectives, shared experiences, and a sense of belonging in their community. They welcomed diversity and openness in their interactions, enriching their lives with new friendships and meaningful connections.

In addition to external changes, Naree and Thana also faced internal shifts in their perspectives and beliefs. They engaged in conversations about personal growth, values alignment, and the evolving nature of their relationship, embracing change as a catalyst for deeper understanding and connection.

One evening, as they sat by the fireplace, Thana shared his reflections on personal growth. "Naree, I've been thinking about how we've grown individually and as a couple," he said, his tone contemplative.

Naree nodded, feeling a sense of resonance. "Change has a way of shaping our perspectives and priorities," she replied, her voice thoughtful.

Their conversation delved into themes of self-discovery, evolving values, and the continuous journey of growth and learning. They embraced change as an opportunity to evolve together, embracing new insights, challenges, and experiences with openness and curiosity.

As they navigated through moments of change, Naree and Thana discovered a deeper sense of resilience, adaptability, and unity in their relationship. They realized that change was not something to fear but a natural part of life's journey—a journey of growth, transformation, and endless possibilities.

One day, as they walked hand in hand through their neighborhood, Naree spoke softly, "Thana, I'm grateful for how we've embraced change and grown stronger together."

Thana smiled, squeezing her hand gently. "Me too," he replied. "Our journey is filled with change, and it's made us who we are today."

Their embrace of change became a testament to their courage, flexibility, and commitment to growth. They knew that every change they faced was an opportunity for deeper connection, resilience, and embracing the beauty of life's unfolding journey.

And as they continued to navigate through life's changes together, Naree and Thana felt a sense of empowerment and readiness for whatever the future held. They knew that with each change, they grew stronger, more resilient, and more deeply connected in their love for each other.

40

Cherishing Memories

As Naree and Thana journeyed through life's changes and embraced growth, they found themselves cherishing moments of nostalgia and reminiscence—memories that reminded them of their journey together, the milestones they had achieved, and the love that had blossomed amidst it all.

One of the ways they cherished memories was through revisiting meaningful places from their past—the cafes where they had their first dates, the parks where they took long walks, and the beaches where they shared moments of laughter and reflection.

One evening, as they sat on a bench overlooking the city skyline, Naree spoke with a smile. "Thana, remember when we used to come here during our early days together?" she reminisced, her eyes sparkling with nostalgia.

Thana nodded, his heart filled with warmth. "Those moments were the beginning of our beautiful journey," he replied, looking at her with love.

Their trip down memory lane became a celebration of their love story, a reminder of the moments that had shaped their relationship and filled their hearts with joy and gratitude.

In addition to revisiting places, Naree and Thana also cherished memories through shared traditions and rituals that held special meaning for them. They celebrated anniversaries with heartfelt gestures, exchanged love letters on special occasions, and created their own traditions that reflected their unique bond.

One anniversary evening, as they dined at their favorite restaurant, Thana surprised Naree with a handwritten letter expressing his love and appreciation. "Naree, this letter is a token of my love for you," he said, handing her the envelope with a smile.

Naree's eyes filled with tears of joy as she read his heartfelt words. "Thana, this means the world to me," she whispered, touched by his gesture.

Their shared traditions became a way to honor their love, create lasting memories, and reaffirm their commitment to each other.

Another way they cherished memories was through creating photo albums and scrapbooks filled with moments captured throughout their journey together. They spent hours flipping through pages, reliving memories, and laughing at the candid moments captured in photographs.

One rainy afternoon, as they curled up on the couch with a photo album, Naree smiled at a picture from their first trip together. "Thana, look at how far we've come," she remarked, her voice filled with nostalgia.

Thana nodded, tracing a finger over the photograph. "Every memory is a treasure," he replied, feeling grateful for their shared experiences.

Their photo albums became a treasure trove of memories—a testament to their love, adventures, and growth as a couple. They cherished each photograph as a reminder of the moments that had woven the tapestry of their love story.

As they continued to cherish memories together, Naree and Thana felt a deep sense of gratitude for the journey they had embarked on—the highs, the lows, and everything in between. They knew that their memories were not just moments frozen in time but a reflection of the love and connection they shared.

One evening, as they sat under the stars, Naree spoke softly, "Thana, our memories are the heartbeats of our love story."

Thana smiled, pulling her close. "Every memory is etched in my heart forever," he replied, savoring the moment of togetherness.

Their journey of cherishing memories became a testament to the beauty of love—a love that grew stronger with each memory, each milestone, and each shared moment of joy and gratitude.

And as they continued to create new memories and cherish old ones, Naree and Thana knew that their love story was a timeless tapestry woven with threads of love, laughter, and cherished memories that would last a lifetime.

41

Embracing Challenges Together

As Naree and Thana continued their journey of love and growth, they encountered challenges that tested their resilience, communication, and commitment to each other. These challenges became opportunities for growth, strengthening their bond and deepening their understanding of love.

One of the challenges they faced was navigating through differences in perspectives and opinions. Despite their strong connection, Naree and Thana realized that they had individual beliefs and viewpoints that sometimes led to conflicts or misunderstandings.

One evening, during a discussion about a topic they disagreed on, Naree and Thana found themselves in a heated argument. Emotions ran high as they both tried to express their thoughts and feelings.

After a moment of tension, Naree took a deep breath and spoke calmly, "Thana, I understand that we have different perspectives, but our love is stronger than any disagreement. Let's find a way to communicate and understand each other better."

Thana nodded, realizing the importance of empathy and open communication. "You're right, Naree. Let's listen to each other without judgment and find common ground," he replied, willing to work through their differences.

Their willingness to navigate through challenges with patience, understanding, and respect strengthened their communication skills and deepened their connection.

Another challenge they encountered was managing external pressures and expectations, particularly from family members and society. As they made decisions about their future together, Naree and Thana faced conflicting opinions and advice from well-meaning but sometimes overwhelming sources.

One afternoon, as they discussed their plans for the future, Naree expressed her concerns about external pressures. "Thana, I want us to make decisions based on our values and dreams, not on what others expect of us," she shared, her voice determined.

Thana agreed, feeling the weight of external expectations. "I'm with you, Naree. Let's stay true to ourselves and our vision for the future," he replied, offering his unwavering support.

Their commitment to staying aligned with their own values and dreams, despite external pressures, became a source of strength and unity in their relationship.

In addition to external challenges, Naree and Thana also faced internal struggles and insecurities that tested their emotional resilience. Moments of self-doubt, fear of failure, and vulnerability surfaced, challenging them to confront their inner demons and find solace in each other's love and support.

One evening, as they sat in quiet reflection, Naree spoke softly about her fears. "Thana, I sometimes doubt myself and worry about the future," she admitted, her voice tinged with vulnerability.

Thana listened with empathy, offering words of encouragement and reassurance. "Naree, you're stronger than you think, and I believe in you. Let's face these challenges together," he replied, his gaze filled with love.

Their shared vulnerability and support for each other's emotional well-being became a cornerstone of their relationship, fostering trust, resilience, and a deep sense of intimacy.

As they embraced challenges together, Naree and Thana realized that every obstacle they faced was an opportunity for growth, learning, and deepening their love. They navigated through disagreements with grace, managed external pressures with resilience, and supported each other through moments of vulnerability and self-doubt.

One day, as they walked hand in hand through a park, Naree spoke with gratitude, "Thana, facing challenges together has made us stronger as a couple."

Thana smiled, pulling her close. "Our love is a source of strength and courage," he replied, cherishing the journey they had embarked on together.

Their journey of embracing challenges together became a testament to the power of love in overcoming obstacles and growing stronger as individuals and as a couple. They knew that no matter what challenges lay ahead, they would face them hand in hand, united in their love and commitment to each other.

And as they continued to navigate through life's challenges and celebrate their victories together, Naree and Thana felt a deep sense of gratitude for the journey they had shared—a journey of love, growth, and unwavering support that had shaped their lives in profound ways.

42

Rediscovering Passion

Amidst the challenges and triumphs of their journey, Naree and Thana found themselves rediscovering passion—rekindling their spark, reigniting their dreams, and embracing the joy of shared passions that brought them closer together.

One of the ways they rediscovered passion was through their shared love for travel and exploration. As they embarked on new adventures and visited breathtaking destinations, they felt a sense of awe and wonder that reignited their sense of adventure and curiosity.

One summer, they decided to take a road trip along the coast, exploring hidden beaches, charming villages, and scenic landscapes. With the wind in their hair and the sun on their faces, Naree and Thana felt a renewed sense of excitement and freedom.

"Thana, I love how travel brings us closer and ignites our sense of adventure," Naree exclaimed, her eyes shining with joy as they watched the sunset over the ocean.

Thana nodded, feeling grateful for their shared experiences. "Every journey with you is a treasure," he replied, cherishing the moments of discovery and connection.

Their shared passion for travel became a source of joy, inspiration, and deeper connection in their relationship.

In addition to travel, Naree and Thana also rediscovered passion through creative collaborations and shared projects. They worked on photography projects together, combining their unique styles and perspectives to create breathtaking visual stories that captured the essence of their love and shared experiences.

One evening, as they reviewed their latest collaborative project, Naree smiled with pride. "Thana, our creative synergy is truly special," she remarked, admiring their work displayed on the screen.

Thana nodded, feeling a sense of accomplishment. "Our shared passion for art and storytelling brings out the best in us," he replied, grateful for their creative bond.

Their creative collaborations became a celebration of their shared passions, talents, and the magic that happened when they worked together as a team.

Another way they rediscovered passion was through nurturing their individual interests and hobbies. Naree delved deeper into her photography, exploring new techniques and themes that spoke to her soul. Thana dedicated time to his writing, crafting stories that reflected his growth, experiences, and dreams.

One rainy afternoon, as they pursued their creative pursuits at home, Naree spoke with enthusiasm. "Thana, I feel so alive when I'm behind the camera, capturing moments that tell a story," she shared, her eyes filled with passion.

Thana nodded, feeling inspired by her dedication. "Writing has become my sanctuary, a space where I can express myself freely," he replied, immersed in his creative flow.

Their commitment to nurturing their passions as individuals enriched their relationship, fostering a sense of fulfillment, purpose, and mutual support.

As they rediscovered passion together, Naree and Thana felt a renewed sense of energy, creativity, and joy in their lives. They knew that their shared passions were not just hobbies but expressions of their love, dreams, and the boundless possibilities of their journey together.

One evening, as they sat under the stars, Naree spoke softly, "Thana, rediscovering passion with you has been a beautiful journey."

Thana smiled, pulling her close. "Our shared passions light up our path and bring us closer together," he replied, savoring the moments of connection and inspiration.

Their journey of rediscovering passion became a testament to the transformative power of love, creativity, and shared dreams. They knew that as long as they nurtured their passions and supported each other's dreams, their love would continue to flourish and inspire them every step of the way.

43

The Power of Gratitude

In the midst of their journey filled with love, challenges, and rediscovery, Naree and Thana realized the profound impact of gratitude—a practice that transformed their perspective, deepened their appreciation for each other, and brought a sense of abundance and joy into their lives.

One of the ways they embraced gratitude was through daily rituals of appreciation and acknowledgment. Each morning, they started their day with gratitude journals, writing down three things they were grateful for, big or small.

"Thana, I'm grateful for the sunrise we witnessed together this morning," Naree shared, her voice filled with warmth as they sat on their balcony, sipping their morning tea.

Thana smiled, nodding in agreement. "I'm grateful for the laughter we shared during breakfast," he replied, cherishing the simple moments of connection and joy.

Their practice of gratitude created a ripple effect of positivity, mindfulness, and a deeper sense of contentment in their relationship.

In addition to daily rituals, Naree and Thana also embraced gratitude through acts of kindness and generosity towards others. They volunteered at local charities, donated to causes they believed in, and expressed appreciation to the people who made a positive impact in their lives.

One weekend, as they volunteered at a community garden, Naree spoke with gratitude. "Thana, seeing the smiles on people's faces when they receive fresh produce brings me so much joy," she remarked, feeling grateful for the opportunity to give back.

Thana nodded, feeling the warmth of their shared purpose. "Our actions of kindness and generosity create a ripple of goodness in the world," he replied, touched by the sense of community they were part of.

Their acts of gratitude and kindness became a way to spread love, positivity, and compassion in their community and beyond.

Another way they embraced gratitude was through moments of reflection and celebration of milestones, achievements, and blessings in their lives. They took time to acknowledge each other's strengths, accomplishments, and the growth they had experienced together.

One evening, as they celebrated a personal milestone, Thana spoke with admiration. "Naree, I'm so proud of how far you've come in your photography career. Your dedication and talent inspire me every day," he expressed, his eyes filled with pride.

Naree smiled, feeling deeply appreciated. "Thana, your support and belief in me mean everything. I'm grateful for our journey together," she replied, touched by his words.

Their moments of reflection and celebration became a reminder of the abundance of love, support, and blessings they shared in their relationship.

As they embraced gratitude in their lives, Naree and Thana felt a profound shift in their perspective—a shift towards seeing the beauty in every moment, appreciating the richness of their experiences, and cultivating a heart full of thankfulness.

One evening, as they watched the sunset, Naree spoke softly, "Thana, gratitude has opened my eyes to the abundance of love and joy in our lives."

Thana nodded, pulling her close. "Every day with you is a gift, and I'm grateful for the love we share," he replied, feeling the warmth of their connection.

Their journey of embracing gratitude became a testament to the power of appreciation, mindfulness, and the transformative impact of a grateful heart. They knew that as long as they embraced gratitude together, their love would continue to grow, deepen, and illuminate their path with joy and abundance.

And as they continued their journey filled with love, challenges, rediscovery, and gratitude, Naree and Thana felt a deep sense of fulfillment and happiness—a happiness rooted in the simple yet profound practice of gratitude that enriched their lives and their love for each other.

44

Navigating Dreams

As Naree and Thana embraced gratitude and cherished their journey together, they found themselves navigating dreams—exploring new horizons, pursuing shared aspirations, and creating a vision for their future that was filled with love, purpose, and possibility.

One of the dreams they navigated together was the vision of a shared home—a space that reflected their personalities, passions, and shared values. They spent weekends visiting potential homes, envisioning their future together, and imagining the memories they would create in each space.

"One day, we'll have a cozy reading nook by the window," Naree remarked, her eyes sparkling with excitement as they toured a charming house.

Thana nodded, picturing their future home filled with love and laughter. "I can imagine us cooking together in this kitchen," he replied, feeling the warmth of their shared dreams.

Their vision of a shared home became a symbol of their commitment, unity, and the dream they were building together.

In addition to their dream of a shared home, Naree and Thana also navigated dreams related to their careers and personal growth. They supported each other's aspirations, offered encouragement during challenges, and celebrated milestones and achievements along the way.

One evening, as they discussed their career goals, Thana expressed his dreams with passion. "Naree, I want to write a book that inspires others and captures the essence of our journey together," he shared, his eyes filled with determination.

Naree smiled, feeling proud of Thana's aspirations. "I'll be by your side, supporting you every step of the way," she replied, offering her unwavering support.

Their shared dreams and aspirations became a source of motivation, inspiration, and a shared sense of purpose in their relationship.

Another dream they navigated together was the vision of a meaningful legacy—a legacy of love, kindness, and positive impact that would extend beyond their lifetime. They discussed ways to give back to their community, support causes they believed in, and leave a lasting legacy of compassion and generosity.

One afternoon, as they volunteered at a local shelter, Naree spoke with a sense of fulfillment. "Thana, I want us to make a difference in people's lives and leave behind a legacy of love and kindness," she expressed, her heart touched by the impact they were making.

Thana nodded, feeling the resonance of their shared vision. "Our legacy is not just what we leave behind but the lives we touch and the hearts we inspire," he replied, grateful for their shared purpose.

Their vision of a meaningful legacy became a driving force in their lives, guiding their actions, decisions, and the way they approached their relationships and contributions to the world.

As they navigated dreams together, Naree and Thana felt a deep sense of alignment, purpose, and fulfillment in their relationship. They knew that their shared dreams were not just aspirations but a reflection of their love, values, and the vision they held for their life together.

One evening, as they stargazed in their backyard, Naree spoke softly, "Thana, navigating dreams with you has been a beautiful journey."

Thana smiled, pulling her close. "Our dreams are the stars that guide us on our journey together," he replied, feeling grateful for the love, dreams, and possibilities they shared.

Their journey of navigating dreams became a testament to the power of vision, unity, and the transformative impact of pursuing shared aspirations and dreams. They knew that as long as they navigated dreams together, their love would continue to flourish, their bond would deepen, and their journey would be filled with purpose, love, and endless possibilities.

45

Finding Balance

Amidst the excitement of pursuing dreams and navigating their journey together, Naree and Thana realized the importance of finding balance—a harmonious blend of work and play, responsibility and relaxation, and personal growth and shared experiences that nurtured their relationship and well-being.

One of the ways they found balance was through mindful practices and self-care routines. They prioritized moments of relaxation, meditation, and rejuvenation, allowing themselves to recharge and reconnect with their inner selves.

One weekend, as they indulged in a spa retreat, Naree spoke with serenity. "Thana, taking time for self-care is essential for our well-being and our relationship," she remarked, feeling the stress melt away.

Thana nodded, feeling the benefits of relaxation. "Mindfulness and self-care help us stay present and appreciate each moment," he replied, savoring the tranquility of their retreat.

Their commitment to finding balance through mindful practices created a foundation of peace, harmony, and emotional well-being in their lives.

In addition to self-care, Naree and Thana also found balance through managing their time and priorities effectively. They created schedules that allowed for work, personal interests, quality time together, and moments of solitude and reflection.

One evening, as they planned their week ahead, Thana spoke with intention. "Naree, finding balance in our time and priorities helps us nurture our relationship and individual growth," he expressed, appreciating the importance of mindful planning.

Naree agreed, feeling the benefits of a balanced schedule. "Our time together is precious, and finding the right balance allows us to make the most of every moment," she replied, grateful for their shared approach to time management.

Their dedication to finding balance in their time and priorities enabled them to create a fulfilling and harmonious life that aligned with their values, goals, and aspirations.

Another way they found balance was through open communication and setting boundaries. They expressed their needs, desires, and limitations honestly, allowing for mutual understanding, respect, and support in their relationship.

One afternoon, as they discussed their boundaries, Naree spoke with clarity. "Thana, communicating our boundaries helps us respect each other's needs and maintain a healthy balance in our relationship," she explained, valuing the importance of clear communication.

Thana nodded, appreciating their open dialogue. "Setting boundaries ensures that we honor ourselves and our relationship," he replied, feeling the strength of their mutual understanding.

Their commitment to open communication and boundaries created a sense of safety, trust, and mutual respect in their relationship, fostering a deep sense of balance and harmony.

As they found balance in their lives and relationship, Naree and Thana felt a sense of peace, fulfillment, and alignment with their true selves. They knew that finding balance was not just about managing time and responsibilities but about nurturing their well-being, their love, and their connection to each other and the world around them.

One evening, as they watched the sunset, Naree spoke softly, "Thana, finding balance with you has brought a sense of harmony and joy into our lives."

Thana smiled, pulling her close. "Our balance is the foundation of our happiness and love," he replied, feeling grateful for the journey they had embarked on together.

Their journey of finding balance became a testament to the power of mindfulness, communication, and self-care in nurturing a harmonious and fulfilling life. They knew that as long as they prioritized balance in their lives and relationship, their love would continue to flourish, their bond would deepen, and their journey would be one of joy, growth, and shared experiences.

46

Embracing Change

As Naree and Thana continued their journey of love and growth, they encountered moments of change—transitions, new beginnings, and transformations that tested their adaptability, resilience, and willingness to embrace the unknown.

One of the changes they faced was a relocation to a new city—a decision that brought excitement, challenges, and opportunities for growth in their lives and relationship. They packed their belongings, said farewell to familiar surroundings, and embarked on a new adventure together.

One evening, as they settled into their new home, Naree spoke with anticipation. "Thana, I'm excited about the possibilities and adventures that await us in this new city," she remarked, feeling a sense of wonder and curiosity.

Thana nodded, embracing the change with optimism. "Every change is an opportunity for growth and new experiences," he replied, feeling the energy of their fresh start.

Their relocation became a symbol of their willingness to embrace change, adapt to new circumstances, and create a life filled with exploration and discovery.

In addition to relocation, Naree and Thana also encountered changes in their careers and personal aspirations. They navigated transitions, explored new opportunities, and supported each other's growth and evolution.

One day, as they discussed their career goals, Thana expressed his aspirations with determination. "Naree, I want to explore new avenues in my writing and take on challenges that push me out of my comfort zone," he shared, his eyes shining with excitement.

Naree smiled, feeling inspired by Thana's courage. "I'll be by your side, cheering you on every step of the way," she replied, offering her unwavering support.

Their openness to change and growth created a sense of adaptability, resilience, and mutual encouragement in their relationship.

Another change they embraced was the evolution of their relationship dynamics—navigating through different phases, roles, and responsibilities as they grew individually and as a couple.

One evening, as they reflected on their journey together, Naree spoke with gratitude. "Thana, our relationship has evolved in beautiful ways, and I'm grateful for the growth we've experienced," she expressed, feeling the depth of their connection.

Thana nodded, cherishing their journey of growth and transformation. "Our love continues to grow and evolve, creating new chapters of our story," he replied, feeling the strength of their bond.

Their willingness to embrace change in their relationship created a sense of depth, intimacy, and shared growth that enriched their connection and love for each other.

As they embraced change together, Naree and Thana realized that every transition, challenge, and transformation was an opportunity for learning, growth, and deepening their bond. They navigated through changes with courage, adaptability, and a sense of adventure that made their journey together even more meaningful and fulfilling.

One evening, as they watched the stars from their balcony, Naree spoke softly, "Thana, embracing change with you has been a journey of growth and discovery."

Thana smiled, pulling her close. "Our willingness to embrace change is a testament to our resilience and love," he replied, feeling grateful for the ever-evolving adventure they shared.

Their journey of embracing change became a reminder of the beauty of transformation, the power of adaptability, and the strength of their love that continued to grow and flourish amidst every new chapter of their lives.

47

Cultivating Compassion

Amidst the changes, challenges, and growth in their journey together, Naree and Thana discovered the profound impact of compassion—a quality that enriched their relationship, deepened their connection, and brought a sense of empathy, understanding, and kindness into their lives.

One of the ways they cultivated compassion was through active listening and empathy. They took time to truly listen to each other's thoughts, feelings, and perspectives, offering support, validation, and a safe space for expression.

One evening, as they shared their thoughts and emotions, Naree spoke with vulnerability. "Thana, I appreciate how you listen to me without judgment and understand what I'm going through," she expressed, feeling seen and heard.

Thana nodded, offering his empathy and presence. "Your feelings matter to me, and I'm here for you always," he replied, embracing her with compassion.

Their practice of active listening and empathy created a foundation of trust, connection, and emotional intimacy in their relationship.

In addition to active listening, Naree and Thana also cultivated compassion through acts of kindness, understanding, and support towards each other and those around them. They volunteered at local charities, offered help to friends in need, and expressed kindness in their daily interactions.

One day, as they volunteered at a homeless shelter, Thana spoke with compassion. "Naree, seeing the gratitude in people's eyes when we offer a helping hand reminds me of the power of compassion," he remarked, touched by the impact of their actions.

Naree smiled, feeling the warmth of their shared kindness. "Compassion is the language of the heart, and it connects us to each other and the world," she replied, grateful for their ability to make a difference.

Their acts of compassion and kindness became a way to spread love, positivity, and healing in their lives and the lives of others.

Another way they cultivated compassion was through forgiveness and understanding. They acknowledged their imperfections, learned from mistakes, and chose to forgive and let go of resentments, fostering a sense of peace and harmony in their relationship.

One afternoon, as they discussed a misunderstanding, Naree spoke with forgiveness. "Thana, I understand where you're coming from, and I forgive you. Our love is stronger than any disagreement," she expressed, choosing compassion over conflict.

Thana nodded, feeling the weight lift off their shoulders. "I'm grateful for your understanding and forgiveness. It brings us closer together," he replied, embracing her with love.

Their practice of forgiveness and understanding created a sense of healing, growth, and deeper connection in their relationship.

As they cultivated compassion together, Naree and Thana felt a profound shift in their relationship—a shift towards greater empathy, understanding, and unconditional love. They knew that as long as they nurtured compassion in their hearts and actions, their love would continue to deepen, their bond would strengthen, and their journey would be filled with kindness, empathy, and grace.

One evening, as they walked hand in hand, Naree spoke softly, "Thana, cultivating compassion with you has opened my heart to a deeper love."

Thana smiled, pulling her close. "Our compassion is a reflection of the love we share, and it brings us closer every day," he replied, feeling the beauty of their shared journey.

Their journey of cultivating compassion became a testament to the transformative power of empathy, kindness, and understanding in nurturing a love that was compassionate, enduring, and truly unconditional.

48

Embracing Vulnerability

As Naree and Thana delved deeper into their journey of love, growth, and compassion, they discovered the courage and strength that came with embracing vulnerability—a quality that allowed them to be authentic, open, and deeply connected in their relationship.

One of the ways they embraced vulnerability was through honest communication and sharing their innermost thoughts, fears, and desires. They created a safe space for vulnerability, where they could express themselves without fear of judgment or rejection.

One evening, as they sat by the fireplace, Naree spoke with vulnerability. "Thana, I want to share something with you that I've been feeling lately," she expressed, her voice soft with honesty.

Thana listened attentively, offering his presence and support. "I'm here for you, Naree. Your vulnerability is what makes our connection so special," he replied, embracing her with love and understanding.

Their willingness to be vulnerable with each other created a deep sense of intimacy, trust, and authenticity in their relationship.

In addition to honest communication, Naree and Thana also embraced vulnerability through taking emotional risks, expressing their needs and boundaries, and allowing themselves to be seen and loved for who they truly were.

One day, as they discussed their dreams and fears, Thana shared his vulnerability. "Naree, I have fears about the future and whether I'll be able to fulfill my aspirations," he admitted, his eyes reflecting his inner turmoil.

Naree held his hand, offering her reassurance and love. "Thana, your vulnerability is a strength, and together, we'll navigate through any challenges that come our way," she replied, feeling the depth of their connection.

Their openness to vulnerability allowed for deeper understanding, empathy, and a sense of shared strength and support in their relationship.

Another way they embraced vulnerability was through accepting their imperfections and embracing self-love and self-compassion. They recognized that vulnerability was not a sign of weakness but a pathway to growth, healing, and deeper connection.

One afternoon, as they practiced self-care together, Naree spoke with self-compassion. "Thana, embracing our vulnerabilities allows us to embrace our humanity and love ourselves fully," she expressed, feeling a sense of liberation.

Thana nodded, embracing his own vulnerability with kindness. "Self-love and self-compassion are the foundations of our relationship," he replied, feeling the beauty of their shared journey.

Their practice of embracing vulnerability and self-love created a sense of wholeness, acceptance, and deep connection with themselves and each other.

As they embraced vulnerability together, Naree and Thana felt a profound sense of freedom, authenticity, and intimacy in their relationship. They knew that vulnerability was not a weakness but a gateway to love, connection, and profound growth.

One evening, as they danced under the stars, Naree spoke softly, "Thana, embracing vulnerability with you has deepened our love in ways I never imagined."

Thana smiled, holding her close. "Our vulnerability is the bridge that connects our hearts and souls," he replied, feeling the depth of their connection.

Their journey of embracing vulnerability became a testament to the power of authenticity, courage, and love in creating a relationship that was genuine, intimate, and truly transformative.

49

Celebrating Growth

Naree and Thana sat on their balcony, surrounded by the gentle rustle of leaves and the soft glow of twilight. As they reflected on their journey of love, vulnerability, and compassion, they realized the beauty and significance of celebrating growth—acknowledging the progress they had made individually and as a couple, and honoring the lessons learned along the way.

"Naree, looking back at where we started and where we are now, I'm amazed at how much we've grown together," Thana said, his voice tinged with awe and gratitude.

Naree nodded, her eyes sparkling with pride. "Yes, Thana. Our journey has been filled with challenges and blessings, but through it all, we've grown stronger, wiser, and more connected," she replied, reflecting on the moments of growth that had shaped their relationship.

Their journey of growth began with the courage to step into vulnerability—to open their hearts, share their fears and dreams, and embrace their authentic selves. This vulnerability allowed them to forge a deep bond built on trust, understanding, and unconditional love.

"I remember the first time I shared my vulnerability with you, Thana. It was scary but also liberating," Naree recalled, feeling a sense of empowerment in owning her truth.

Thana smiled, recalling the moment vividly. "Your vulnerability brought us closer together and paved the way for our growth as individuals and as partners," he remarked, grateful for the depth of their connection.

Their willingness to embrace vulnerability became a catalyst for personal and relational growth—a journey of self-discovery, acceptance, and continuous learning.

As they navigated the ups and downs of life, Naree and Thana encountered moments of change and transition—relocations, career shifts, and new beginnings that tested their resilience, adaptability, and commitment to each other.

"I never imagined we would relocate to a new city and start afresh, but that change brought us closer and expanded our horizons," Thana shared, reminiscing about their adventurous spirit and willingness to embrace new experiences.

Naree nodded, feeling grateful for the opportunities that change had brought into their lives. "Change challenged us to grow, adapt, and discover new aspects of ourselves and our relationship," she added, cherishing the lessons learned along the way.

Their journey of growth also included moments of celebration—milestones, achievements, and shared victories that highlighted their progress and accomplishments.

"Remember when we celebrated your book launch, Thana? It was a testament to your hard work, dedication, and creativity," Naree said, recalling the joyous occasion filled with love and support.

Thana nodded, feeling a sense of fulfillment in realizing his dream. "Your unwavering belief in me and our shared celebrations made every achievement even more meaningful," he replied, grateful for Naree's constant support.

Their celebrations became a way to honor their growth, resilience, and shared success—a reminder of the strength and unity they had cultivated in their journey together.

In addition to personal growth, Naree and Thana experienced relational growth—navigating challenges, resolving conflicts, and deepening their understanding and communication with each other.

"Our journey wasn't always smooth, but every challenge brought us closer and taught us valuable lessons in patience, empathy, and compromise," Naree reflected, acknowledging the growth that came from overcoming obstacles together.

Thana agreed, emphasizing the importance of growth in their relationship. "Our ability to learn and grow from our experiences has strengthened our bond and deepened our love for each other," he added, appreciating the depth of their connection.

Their journey of growth extended beyond themselves and their relationship—it encompassed their impact on others, their contributions to their community, and their commitment to making a positive difference in the world.

"I'm proud of how we've used our growth and experiences to uplift others, contribute to meaningful causes, and spread love and kindness wherever we go," Thana remarked, reflecting on their shared values and impact.

Naree smiled, feeling a sense of purpose in their collective efforts. "Our growth isn't just for ourselves—it's a gift we share with others, inspiring hope, resilience, and compassion," she replied, grateful for the opportunity to make a difference.

Their journey of growth became a testament to the transformative power of love, resilience, and continuous learning—a journey marked by courage, vulnerability, and the unwavering belief in the potential for growth and positive change.

As they sat together, basking in the glow of their shared journey, Naree and Thana felt a deep sense of gratitude, fulfillment, and excitement for the adventures that lay ahead—a future filled with endless possibilities, new experiences, and the enduring strength of their love and growth together.

50

Embracing Life's Seasons

As Naree and Thana continued their journey of love and growth, they came to realize the beauty and wisdom in embracing life's seasons—the ebb and flow of change, transformation, and renewal that enriched their relationship and deepened their connection with each passing day.

They found inspiration in the natural world around them, witnessing the cycles of seasons—spring bringing new beginnings, summer radiating warmth and joy, autumn painting a canvas of change and reflection, and winter offering a time of rest, introspection, and preparation for new growth.

One evening, as they walked through a serene garden, Naree marveled at the beauty of nature's seasons. "Thana, each season has its own magic and lessons to teach us about life and love," she remarked, feeling a sense of wonder and gratitude.

Thana nodded, appreciating the wisdom in nature's rhythms. "Just like the seasons, our relationship experiences different phases of growth, challenges, and renewal, shaping us into who we are today," he replied, reflecting on the journey they had shared.

Their observation of life's seasons became a metaphor for their own experiences—moments of blossoming love, vibrant joy, introspective growth, and resilient renewal that mirrored the changing landscapes of nature.

One of the lessons they learned from embracing life's seasons was the importance of adaptability and resilience—being able to navigate through transitions, challenges, and unexpected changes with grace, strength, and a sense of purpose.

"We've faced our share of storms and sunny days, but through it all, we've learned to adapt, grow, and find beauty in every season of our lives," Naree shared, recalling the challenges they had overcome together.

Thana agreed, acknowledging the resilience that had strengthened their bond. "Our ability to weather life's seasons has made us stronger, more compassionate, and deeply appreciative of the journey we've shared," he added, feeling a sense of pride in their growth.

Their journey of embracing life's seasons also included moments of reflection and gratitude—taking time to pause, appreciate the present moment, and express gratitude for the blessings, lessons, and experiences that had shaped their relationship.

"Amidst life's hustle and bustle, it's important to pause, reflect, and express gratitude for the love, joy, and growth we've experienced together," Naree said, feeling a sense of peace and contentment in the simple moments of connection.

Thana nodded, savoring the beauty of their shared reflections. "Gratitude reminds us of the abundance in our lives and deepens our appreciation for each other and the journey we're on," he remarked, grateful for Naree's presence and love.

Their practice of reflection and gratitude became a source of strength, joy, and perspective—a reminder to cherish the journey, celebrate the milestones, and embrace the ever-changing seasons of life and love.

In addition to adaptability and gratitude, Naree and Thana also learned the importance of balance and harmony—nurturing their relationship, personal growth, and shared aspirations while honoring their individual dreams, passions, and identities.

"Our journey has taught us the value of balance—balancing our love for each other with our personal growth, dreams, and aspirations," Naree expressed, recognizing the importance of maintaining harmony in their lives.

Thana nodded, embracing the concept of balance in their relationship. "Finding harmony allows us to thrive individually and as a couple, creating a foundation of mutual support, understanding, and fulfillment," he replied, feeling the equilibrium they had achieved.

Their pursuit of balance and harmony became a guiding principle in their lives—a way to navigate through life's complexities, stay connected to their core values, and foster a sense of unity and purpose in their relationship.

As they embraced life's seasons together, Naree and Thana found joy, wisdom, and a deeper sense of connection in every phase of their journey. They knew that just like the changing seasons, their love would continue to evolve, flourish, and bloom in new and beautiful ways, each season bringing its own gifts, lessons, and blessings.

51

Embracing the Infinite Journey

As Naree and Thana approached the culmination of their journey together, they reflected on the infinite nature of love—the timeless, boundless, and ever-evolving essence that had woven their lives into a tapestry of beauty, growth, and profound connection.

"Our journey has been a testament to the infinite nature of love—a love that knows no limits, transcends time and space, and continues to deepen with each passing moment," Naree mused, her voice filled with awe and reverence.

Thana nodded in agreement, his eyes reflecting the depth of their shared experiences. "Love has been the guiding force in our journey—a force that has shaped us, transformed us, and brought us closer to each other and to ourselves," he replied, feeling the profound impact of their love.

Their reflection on the infinite nature of love led them to explore the concept of interconnectedness—the interconnected threads that bound their hearts, souls, and destinies together in a dance of unity and harmony.

"As we navigate through life's twists and turns, I'm reminded of the invisible threads that connect us—the threads of destiny, fate, and divine timing that have brought us together in this beautiful journey," Naree expressed, feeling a sense of wonder at the intricacies of their connection.

Thana smiled, feeling the resonance of their interconnectedness. "Our souls are intertwined in a dance of love and purpose—a dance that transcends the boundaries of time and space, weaving a story of eternal devotion and profound connection," he remarked, embracing the depth of their bond.

Their exploration of interconnectedness also brought them to the realization of the power of intention—the intention to love, to grow, and to create a life filled with meaning, purpose, and joy.

"Our intentions have guided us on this journey—they've shaped our choices, our actions, and our shared vision for the future," Naree reflected, recognizing the importance of aligning their intentions with their values and dreams.

Thana nodded, feeling the alignment of their intentions. "Our intention to love fiercely, to grow continuously, and to create a life of purpose and fulfillment has brought us to this moment—a moment of gratitude, clarity, and deep connection," he replied, embracing the power of their shared intentions.

Their journey of intentionality and interconnectedness became a celebration of the infinite possibilities that love, growth, and unity offered—a journey that transcended the confines of time and space, inviting them to embrace the richness and depth of their shared experiences.

As they embraced the infinite nature of their journey, Naree and Thana felt a sense of completion and wholeness—a deep knowing that their love story would continue to unfold in endless ways, each chapter revealing new depths of understanding, joy, and purpose.

"One chapter may be ending, but our love story is infinite—it's a story that will continue to evolve, expand, and inspire us to new heights of love and connection," Naree said, her voice filled with optimism and hope for the future.

Thana nodded, feeling the eternal nature of their love. "Our journey together is a testament to the power of love—a love that knows no bounds, transcends all obstacles, and lights up the path ahead with infinite possibilities," he replied, embracing Naree with a renewed sense of gratitude and love.

And so, as the sun set on one chapter of their journey, Naree and Thana embraced the infinite possibilities that lay before them—a future filled with love, growth, and the timeless beauty of their shared connection—a connection that would continue to weave their lives together in a tapestry of infinite love and joy, forever and always.

52

A New Beginning

As Naree and Thana stood at the threshold of a new chapter in their lives, they felt a mix of excitement, anticipation, and gratitude for the journey they had shared and the adventures that awaited them.

"Our journey has been filled with moments of love, growth, and discovery, and now, we stand on the brink of a new beginning—a fresh start filled with endless possibilities," Naree said, her eyes shining with hope and determination.

Thana nodded, feeling the energy of new beginnings. "This new chapter is a chance for us to embrace change, follow our dreams, and continue growing together in love and harmony," he replied, envisioning the bright future that lay ahead.

Their conversation about new beginnings led them to reflect on the lessons they had learned and the values that had guided them throughout their journey.

"As we embark on this new chapter, let's carry forward the lessons of resilience, compassion, and gratitude that have shaped our relationship," Naree suggested, emphasizing the importance of staying true to their core values.

Thana agreed wholeheartedly. "Our commitment to love, growth, and authenticity has been the foundation of our journey, and it will continue to guide us as we step into this new phase of life," he affirmed, feeling a sense of purpose and clarity.

Their reflection on values and lessons learned was accompanied by a sense of readiness—a readiness to embrace change, take on new challenges, and create a life filled with purpose and meaning.

"Change can be daunting, but it also brings opportunities for growth, exploration, and new experiences," Naree said, acknowledging the mix of emotions that often accompanied transitions.

Thana nodded, feeling the excitement of stepping into the unknown. "Let's embrace change with open hearts and open minds, trusting in our resilience and the strength of our bond," he suggested, offering Naree a reassuring smile.

Their conversation about readiness and openness to change sparked a sense of adventure—a desire to explore new horizons, chase their dreams, and create a life that reflected their deepest passions and aspirations.

"As we embark on this new chapter, let's dare to dream big, take bold steps, and live our lives with passion and purpose," Naree proposed, her eyes filled with determination and enthusiasm.

Thana grinned, feeling the thrill of possibility. "Let's make this new beginning a chapter filled with laughter, love, and unforgettable moments—a chapter that we'll look back on with joy and gratitude," he exclaimed, ready to embrace the journey ahead.

Their shared vision for the future was one of growth, connection, and fulfillment—a vision that encompassed their individual dreams and shared aspirations, weaving them into a tapestry of endless possibilities.

"Here's to new beginnings, to following our hearts, and to creating a life that reflects the depth of our love and the beauty of our shared journey," Naree toasted, raising her glass in celebration.

Thana joined her in the toast, his eyes reflecting the excitement and determination in his heart. "To new adventures, to seizing every moment, and to building a future filled with love, laughter, and endless possibilities," he echoed, feeling the warmth of Naree's hand in his.

And so, with hearts full of hope, courage, and love, Naree and Thana stepped into their new beginning—a chapter waiting to be written with love, passion, and the infinite possibilities that life had in store for them, forever and always.

Forever And Always

As we reach the end of "Eternal Love in Bangkok: Naree and Thana's Journey," the echoes of love, growth, and eternal devotion linger in our hearts. Through the twists and turns of their journey, Naree and Thana have shown us the transformative power of love—a power that transcends time, space, and every obstacle in its path.

In the final pages of this book, we are reminded of the enduring beauty of true love—the kind of love that knows no bounds, no limitations, and no endings. Naree and Thana's story may have reached its conclusion, but their love will continue to inspire and uplift us, reminding us that true love, once found, lasts forever and always.

As we bid farewell to these beloved characters, let us carry with us the lessons of resilience, compassion, and unwavering commitment that they have taught us. May their love story serve as a beacon of hope, a celebration of human connection, and a testament to the enduring power of love.

With gratitude and love,
Mikey Katodiya

Also by Mikey Katodiya

Love Stories Around the World
Long-Distance Love in New York
Eternal Love in Bangkok

Standalone
Yesterday's Love Story

About the Author

Meet, who often goes by the pen name "Mikey," is a passionate writer who believes in the power of storytelling to inspire and heal. Writing has been his creative outlet, allowing him to explore complex emotions and share them with others. 'Yesterday's Love Story' is his debut work, born frompersonal experiences and a desire to connect with readers on a deeply emotional level. Meet hopes his words, written under the pen nameMikey, will resonate with those seeking solace and strength in the face of adversity.

Read more at https://www.instagram.com/bigpicstory.